MONSTROUS TALES – VOLUME 2
A Horror Anthology of
Longer Stories For A Satisfying Read

I0554584

Edited by Dorothy Davies

MONSTROUS TALES – VOLUME 2
A Horror Anthology of
Longer Stories For A Satisfying Read

GRAVESTONE PRESS

CONTENTS

CONTENTS

Woodenhead Haunts My Dreams
David Turnbull

I am haunted by Woodenhead. He fills my nights and invades my reality. Woodenhead, you ask. Who or what is Woodenhead? I'm going to tell you. Whether you believe a word of it is entirely up to you.

If you grew up in the UK in the late 60's and early 70's, as I did, you'll recall that the BBC used to show kids' TV programs from other parts of Europe. They were mostly in black and white, sometimes with subtitles, but more often quite badly dubbed into English and supplemented by a narration in English as a fall back in case you didn't quite manage to follow the plot.

Some of these shows were downright weird and pretty damn scary. Take the Singing Ringing Tree. It was based on a dark fairy tale by the brothers Grimm called Hurleburlebutz. The BBC broadcast it regularly between 1964 and 1980. It has often been described as the scariest children's TV series ever.

I don't agree with that assessment.

To my mind the crown goes unequivocally to Woodenhead.

Almost everyone I've ever mentioned Woodenhead to thinks I burdened myself with a false memory. But I vividly recall myself curled up and terrified, in an armchair in my parents' house watching it play out on the TV screen. My big brother Jeff sprawled out on the sofa, hurling insults at me for being such a cry baby.

I confronted Jeff numerous times about Woodenhead during his life and how we'd watched it together. He always denied ever having seen it. Like everyone else he said I was imagining something that never happened. I knew he was lying. Whenever I spoke to him about Woodenhead his upper lip would gleam with sweat.

For a few years, when I was in my early to mid-twenties, I was told in no uncertain terms that I was Schizophrenic. The psychiatric doctor who handed down this diagnosis told me that bizarre beliefs, delusions and hallucinations were classic symptoms of Schizophrenia.

She claimed that Woodenhead seemed undeniably real to me because my condition ran so deep. She said my subconscious was clearly covering for some traumatic experience I had endured in my childhood around the time I believed I had watched Woodenhead.

I asked Jeff if he remembered anything that happened in our family that I might have blanked out and replaced with a false memory. He couldn't think of a single thing. As far as he was concerned, we had a normal suburban childhood.

My doctor said whatever had happened to trigger my Schizophrenia was likely to be buried pretty deep within my psyche. For a while she even managed to convince me that she was right. After all there was no evidence to prove that Woodenhead had ever existed. By then I had a letter signed by the head of BBC Children's Entertainment categorically denying that such a program had ever been broadcast by the Corporation.

My doctor told me to write down what I recalled about this *phantom of my mind* (her words) so that she and I could try to work out if it held any clues. I bought a little notebook, mined my memories and the filled the lined pages with every detail. I will recount here what I wrote, the comments and observations are recent additions.

Woodenhead
A children's TV series
Shown in the summer of 1972

Episode One - *introduces us to Gustav the woodcutter and his mischievous son, Jürgen.*

Jürgen is always getting into trouble with the villagers while his father is off in the woods chopping down trees.

Gustav decides it is time Jürgen is taught some responsibility so he gives him his spare axe and takes him into the woods to impart to him the art of tree felling.

Naughty Jürgen wanders off and loses his axe. He sits down for a rest. He falls asleep.

*When he wakes, he finds himself surrounded by a pack of wolves. (*As I recall these wolves were actually a bunch of filthy looking, unshaven actors with bad teeth and flea-bitten costumes. When I was ten this just made them all the more terrifying.)

When Jürgen sees the wolves, he lets out a yell and goes fleeing through the trees. The wolves give chase, howling and growling. Jürgen trips on a branch and smashes his head on a rock. The wolves set about devouring his legs.

Just when you think he will surely be eaten alive Gustav charges the wolves and chases them off with his axe. The show ends with Gustav carrying his son's bloodied body through the trees.

Episode Two - Gustav is so overcome with grief that he takes a huge cart of kindling to the witch's hut deep in the darkest part of the woods. In exchange for the kindling she agrees to give Gustav the wherewithal to bring Jürgen back to life. She grinds a magical potion of dark, sooty dust in her mortar and pestle and whispers into Gustav's ear what must be done.

Back home Gustav shaves a slice from a hunk of wood and uses panel pins to nail this to the deep, dented wound on Jürgen's head. Then he removes the back from his rocking chair, takes his axe and chops off Jürgen's gnawed and mangled legs. This horrendous amputation scene is shown as an eerie silhouette of Gustav, cast against the wall by the flicker of the fire in the hearth, axe raised high above his head and sweeping in a downward motion.

Following the witch's instructions Gustav uses his tools to attach the remainder of Jürgen's body to the seat of the dismantled rocker. Then he takes the witch's powder and sprinkles it over his dead son. The background music rises to a crescendo.

Jürgen's eyes snap open.

"Papa! I'm alive!" he goes. (His voice is dubbed into English and the words don't quite

10

synchronize with the movement of his lips. This accentuates creepiness of the scene.)

Jürgen begins to laugh as he rocks back and forth. The camera pans in and out in time with him. You can see the blood that oozes from the nail holes in the wooden repair to his head.

He rocks
He laughs
He rocks
He laughs
"I'm alive. I'm alive."

(It is this image more than any other that haunts my nightmares. This is also mainly the manner in which Woodenhead manifests himself in what has been described as my frequent hallucinatory episodes.)

Episode Three - *commences with Jürgen learning to get around by rocking back and forth and putting the rockers on the chair into motion.*

He rocks his way to the village and waves happily to the stunned villagers. On the way home he rocks past a field and calls out to a shepherd tending his flock. When the sheep see him, they stampede over the nearest hill, much to the shepherd's consternation. Back home he rocks around the yard, chasing geese and chickens, laughing all the way.

What he doesn't realize is that he is being spied upon by a little band of robbers. They are watching him through a telescope, passing it back and forth between each other. There are four of them, played by the same filthy, unshaven actors who played the pack of wolves, only now they are dressed like gypsies, rather than in the mangy wolf costumes.

When Gustav sets off into the woods with his axe slung over his shoulder, the robbers rush down to the cottage and kidnap Jürgen. They lift him up, rocking chair runners resting on their shoulders, like they are carrying a Prince in his sedan. Jürgen screams and wails for his father. The final shot fades out to the robbers hefting Jürgen away into the distance while chanting a discordant little rhyme.

Hiddle Diddle
Hearts full of joy
Today we have stolen
A wooden headed boy

(I have to confess that rhyme burrows into my head like an earworm so often that it drives me to distraction and destroys my attention levels. It's played a huge part in me never being able hold down a decent job.)

Episode Four - *the robbers have Jürgen locked up in cage on horse drawn trailer that they transport from town to town. They advertise him as Woodenhead, the Rocking Chair Boy and charge an entry fee for people to come and see him.* (In the show the words on the sign are in a foreign language with subtitles as an explanation. It taxes me severely trying to remember those words. Because finding out what language they were written in might be a huge clue as to the program's origins.)

Jürgen, or Woodenhead, sulks in his rocking chair whenever the curtain is pulled back to reveal the cage. The ugliest of the robbers has to constantly poke him with a long stick to get him to rock back and forth. When they see this the audiences mock him and call him a monster.

But word gets out and more and more people come to see him.

The money starts rolling in for the robbers.

One day the witch from the woods pays a visit. She realizes that this is the son of the kindly woodcutter who fetched her kindling in exchange for a potion. She sneaks a little knife into Woodenhead's hand and whispers that it has magical properties which will help him escape if he slashes it through the air.

That night, alone in the cage, behind the closed curtain, Woodenhead begins to rock back and forth. He takes the knife and slashes it through the air. Immediately a tear appears on the TV screen. Woodhead laughs. He rocks and slashes, rocks and slashes. And with each slash the tear grows wider and wider. Till finally on the last slash his mended head comes right out of the TV screen and into your room, laughing maniacally.

(I have no idea how they achieved this effect. It was long before computer generated CGI or 3D television. All I know is that Woodhead came straight through the TV screen. I remember screaming. I remember my brother, who was sitting on the floor, yelping and kicking frantically back with his heels to get out of the way.)

This is where the episode ends.

13

There was no Episode Five – although I was sure back then that there was supposed to be. It's engraved into my memory that the continuity announcer specifically stated that it was a five-part serial before the start of each episode.

I remember coming home from school to find Jeff watching a repeat of a science fiction serial call Mandog. "Turn it to the BBC," I said. I was dreading watching episode five. I'd been having nightmares all week. But I was gripped by a morbid fascination. I simply had to know how the story ended.

Jeff threw a cushion at me. "This is BBC, twat!"

"I can't be. It's supposed to be Woodenhead. The last episode."

"Wooden what?" said Jeff.

This was his first denial.

"Woodenhead," I repeated. "We've been watching it for the past four weeks."

Jeff's face seemed to drain of colour. "I've no idea what you're talking about."

I dropped to my knees and pressed the first button on the TV, just to make sure he wasn't actually watching another channel. "This can't be right," I said. "It's supposed to be Woodenhead. It's supposed to be the last episode."

Jeff pushed me out of the way. "You're round the twist," he yelled at me.

I stood up. "Woodenhead!" I yelled back at him. "The episode last week scared you so much you almost pissed your pants."

Jeff was thirteen at the time and wasn't to be messed with. He glared at me eye to eye. "What did you just say?"

"Woodenhead," I told him. "The rocking chair boy."

I saw his fist clench and if I hadn't managed to turn my head the punch would have hit me hard on the nose. As it was it made contact my cheek, knocked me sideways and caused me to bang my head hard against the wall.

"Never mention the name Woodenhead in front of me again," spat Jeff, twisting his hand into my school shirt and pulling me right up to his face. "If you do, I'll knock your teeth straight down your throat."

That night Woodhead made his first visitation to my room. I woke in the darkness and I could hear the robbers' little chant inside my head.

Hiddle Diddle
Hearts full of joy
Today we have stolen
A wooden headed boy

I checked my watch. Twenty to one in the morning. I gradually became aware of a noise in the room. Something creaking and cricking, creaking and cricking, creaking and cricking. Faster and faster.

When I looked, he was there at the bottom of my bed. Woodhead. Blood had congealed around the nails that attached the piece of wood his father used to repair his head. Flaps of black flesh pinned to the seat of the rocker held him firmly in place. He grinned as he rocked back and forth and slashed his little magical knife through the air. I screamed so loud and for so long my parents were convinced one of the neighbours would report them to social services.

***

"Are you on a nostalgia trip?" asked the assistant behind the counter. She seemed a little young to be working in a charity shop. Her smile was genuine, anything but fake.

Look In was a British magazine which came out in the 70's. It was dedicated to children's TV. I glanced at the stack of six *Look In* annuals I'd discovered in a tattered cardboard box at the back of the shop. I was hoping against hope that somewhere, hidden in one of the pages would be a reference to Woodenhead.

"I'm researching for an article I want to write." It was as good a lie as any.

The assistant looked at the picture cover of the annual at the top of the pile. "I used to love Follyfoot," she said. "And the Tomorrow People and Junior Showtime. All of them really."

The books were 50p each. She rang them into the till and I handed her £3.

"Is the article about anything in particular?" she asked.

"Woodenhead," I replied.

She smiled again. There was a warmth there that I wasn't quite used to. I felt a little awkward as I bundled the books under my arm. "Can't say I remember that one," she said. "But then again, Ben, you are a couple of years older than me."

I cocked my head and looked at her. "You know me?"

She pushed her hair back behind her ears. "We went to the same high school. You were two years above me." She blushed. "When I was twelve, I had such a crush on you."

I didn't know what to say. During my school years I was oblivious to everything going on around me, struggling with nightmares and insomnia. The fact that anyone might have actually had a crush on me was a complete revelation.

She held out her hand.

"Susan Harris."

The name didn't ring any particular bells. But when I shook her hand that smile spread naturally over her face again. "You could invite me for a coffee and tell all about this article you're planning to write."

So began the one and only romantic interlude in my life. It lasted a month and it was over on the very night it should, by rights, have progressed into something real and tangible.

Over a period of three weeks I'd met her after work on half a dozen occasions. We'd gone to a little café on the high street. I shared a sanitized version of the mystery of Woodenhead. How there was no record of its transmission and how, through my fictitious 'article' I intended to prove everyone wrong.

"You're like a detective," she'd say. "It's kind of exciting."

If she'd have had the slightest inkling of the whole truth of the matter, I guess she'd have run a mile to get clear of the madness. In a way that's pretty much what she did eventually do. I suppose it was inevitable. My biggest regret is that it happened a lot sooner than I would have wanted.

Lacking experience in these matters I wasn't at all sure if our little coffee liaisons could legitimately be described as dates. I eventually plucked up the courage to ask her out for a meal. She flashed me that smile of hers, reached out and touched my hand and said, "I'd love to, Ben."

Trattoria Roma was Jeff's recommendation. Unlike me he was quite the lady's man. "Great place for a date." He winked. "Not too busy. Romantic background music. If that doesn't get her in the mood for love, nothing will."

I bought a new shirt and expensive aftershave. On Jeff's advice I also brought along a single red rose. When I handed it to Susan she smiled and kissed me on my cheek. The touch of her lips on my skin felt electric.

The meal went well. Susan ordered chicken carbonara. Being less adventurous I had the lasagne. She looked beautiful. She'd had waves put in her hair and wore a floral blouse, open at the neck to reveal a little heart shaped pendant. It buoyed my confidence that she seemed to be making as much of an effort for me as I was for her.

Half way through the meal she reached over and touched my hand. Our fingers entwined. Our eyes met. My breath caught in my throat. No one had ever looked into my eyes on such an intimate level. This was it. The real thing.

Then I became aware of the music that was playing in the background. A mournful tune played on violin. I recognized it straight away. It was the music that faded in as the theme at the start of each episode of Woodenhead. And faded out at the end during the closing credits. Snatches of it also crept in and out during some of the key scenes in each episode.

I felt sweat go trickling down my back. The image of Woodenhead rocking back and forth flooded my head and destroyed the moment. I snatched my hand back so forcefully I knocked the bread basket from the table. Susan gasped in shock and rubbed her fingers.

"What is this music?" I called to our waiter.

He came attentively to our table.

"Pardon, sir?"

"The music?" I repeated. "What is this music?"

He looked confused.

"Music?"

"That music!" I yelled, rising to my feet and knocking over the chair. "The theme to Woodenhead."

The waiter's mouth dropped open.

"Woodenhead?"

The dreary sound of the violin was making my heart thump in my chest. I began to tremble. The manager came over. "What seems to be the trouble, sir?"

"Trouble?" I yelled. "I'll tell you what the trouble is. This fool doesn't seem to understand a simple question."

The manager looked at the waiter. The waiter shrugged in complete confusion. "What was the question, sir?" asked the manager. "Perhaps I can answer. We don't want any trouble."

Inside my head Woodenhead was grotesquely rocking back and forth and rocking back and forth and rocking back and forth. I grabbed the manager by his neck tie. "The music. I want to know what that damned music is called." From the corner of my eye I saw Susan grabbing her coat and rushing to the door, tears in her eyes. Guests at other tables were looking me in disgust and shaking their heads.

The music came to a sudden halt.

"Paganini's Sonata number 6," said a woman's voice.

When I looked behind the bar one of the waitresses was holding up a c60 cassette.

"Paganini's Sonata number 6," she repeated.

I released my grip on the manager.

"Well thank you," I said. "That's all I wanted to know. It was a simple fucking question."

Just then two police officers rushed through the door.

***

Jeff died when he was only thirty-six. A couple of years earlier he'd set himself up as a roofing contractor. Made a pretty good go of it. One day, not long after Easter, a sudden gust of wind caused

20

him to lose his balance while making repairs to the roof of a three-story town house. He hit the scaffolding several times on the way down and died on impact with the courtyard.

He was married with a four-year-old son and a two-year-old daughter.

I was a hopeless uncle, vacillating between my obsession with Woodhead and my increased dependence on a cocktail of medication to keep me anchored. Sleepless nights, listening endlessly to Paganini's Sonata, dreading the moment that Woodhead would manifest himself, cowering beneath the covers when he did.

I'd never quite gotten over how I'd blown it with Susan Harris. After that dreadful night she'd refused to return any of my calls and had me escorted out of the charity shop by her supervisor the couple of times I'd attempted to visit her at work.

The funeral was dire. A widow and two orphans, my mum almost overwhelmed with grief over the loss of her eldest son, me spaced out on sedatives. All I could think about when they lowered my brother's coffin into the ground was that the only other person who could possibly have confirmed the existence of Woodenhead was about to be buried under six feet of damp soil.

A week or so after the ceremony Jeff's wife, Penny, invited me for dinner and asked if I'd like to look through his belongings for any keepsakes that I might want to lay claim to. Apparently, there were boxes of stuff in the garage from his teenage years.

It turned out to be mostly old vinyl records and cassette tapes. A stamp collection in an album, which may have been worth something. A couple of dented silver cups from his brief dalliance with cross country running. Some wrinkled soccer programs. None of it really struck a chord with me.

I was about to give up when I noticed a pile of drawing sketch pads in a corner, bound in string and covered in dust and cobwebs. Jeff had been quite artistic. I recalled a drawing of his tacked to the wall in our bedroom. Batman socking it to the Riddler - a huge red and yellow *Kapow!* above their heads.

I sat cross legged on the floor and placed the books on my lap so I could blow away the dust and untie the strings. The first pad was filled with superheroes, Captain America, Iron Man and suchlike, diligently hand copied from cells in the comic books we'd both loved reading. The second was full of some pretty good caricatures of the pop and rock stars he'd once idolized - Bowie and Bolan. Steve Harley, Freddie Mercury.

The third had all the pages taped shut. The tape had turned ochre with age and was so brittle to the touch it just dissolved beneath my fingers to a sticky dust. It was easy to wedge it open. It flopped wide across my knees like a dead moth.

I almost screamed out loud at what I saw before me on the page. Woodenhead. Grinning maniacally, slashing the witch's knife and coming straight out of the screen of an old-fashioned looking analogue TV set. Just the way he had at the end of episode four, all those years ago.

Sweat gushed from my brow. I flicked back through the pages. Every page depicted a scene from Woodenhead. Jürgen being chased by the wolves, his legs being devoured by the wolves. Gustav at the witch's cottage, Gustav with his axe raised high, ready to transform his son into Woodenhead. Jürgen as Woodenhead, the Rocking Chair Boy, locked inside the robber's cage.

Each drawing was sketched in charcoal, as if Jeff was somehow trying to recreate the feel and sombre mood of a TV show going out in monochrome. I slammed the pages shut and thumped at my brow with the heel of my hand. He'd lied. All these years, Jeff had lied. I knew it. He had seen Woodenhead after all. Here was the evidence, laid out in vivid detail.

I stumbled to my feet, placed the drawing book between the other two and tried to compose myself as I tucked them under my arm. When I went back into the house through the adjoining door Penny was in the kitchen making a pot of tea and setting out some digestive biscuits on a side plate.

"Do you mind if I have these?" I asked.

"Of course not," she said. "I told you to take anything you wanted.

She came and hugged me. "Look after yourself, won't you, Ben?" obviously far more attuned to my emotional state that I ever was to hers.

***

I stopped taking the medication. Schizophrenia wasn't just a misdiagnosis. It was an insult. I didn't

23

create some sort of wild delusion to cover up a traumatic event. Woodenhead was real. He himself was the traumatic event. He still was the traumatic event. Jeff's drawings were the proof I needed to give me validation.

Woodenhead's nocturnal manifestations would often last not much more than a minute. But a minute is a long, long time when you are scared witless. And without sleeping pills I sometimes had to endure as many as four manifestations in a single night. Dreams last longer. They stay with you till dawn and the residue taints your waking thoughts.

Social media became my new medication. I was quick to latch on to Friends Reunited. I toyed with the notion that perhaps the event that brought Woodenhead to our television was localized. If Jeff saw it and simply taped all his memories up inside that drawing book, then maybe there were others in our area who'd had similar experiences. All I had to do was coax them out.

I posted pictures of some of Jeff's drawing, shared them with people who'd been in my year at school and people I knew through Jeff who had been in Jeff's year. Spread the net wider to other school groupings from our area. Even dared to include Susan Harris in my trawl.

I came up blank. Most people didn't even acknowledge the post. Some responded to my question *'does anyone remember Woodenhead?'* with a straightforward *'nope',* or a variation on *'can't say I do'.* Susan didn't respond at all. I never really expected her to.

For a while I had this nagging idea that maybe it was all a huge wind up on Jeff's part. Maybe he'd created Woodenhead from his own imagination. Maybe he'd shown me the sketches and convinced me that we'd watched the show together.

In my befuddled state it seemed as equally probable as it did improbable.

But then again, why hadn't he brought it to its obvious conclusion? The whole point of a wind up, even one as convoluted as that, was to make a big revelation and laugh your socks off at the other person's reaction when the penny drops. It's what Jeff would have done. He surely wouldn't have kept the deception going long into adulthood. And he definitely wouldn't have prolonged it once he saw the effect it was having on my mental health. Jeff had a dark sense of humour, but not that dark.

I progressed from Friends Reunited to Facebook and, along the way, Twitter and Instagram and all the other variations. I joined lots of groups which exchanged nostalgia about 60's and 70's television. I pretty much stuck to the same mode of operation, posting pictures of Jeff's sketches and asking if anyone remember Woodenhead. I pretty much drew the same negative responses.

Then, three months ago, gradually approaching 50 years since my childhood self had watched a TV show no one else accepted was real, I had a message via a Facebook group called *Stuff of Nightmares*. The premise was simple. People posted about things that had given them nightmares as a child. The message indicated that someone had responded to a post I had put up in the group about six weeks earlier.

I braced myself for yet another disappointment when I went to group's page. The message was from someone called Morag Donaldson. It read simply – *"I remember."* Heart racing, I typed a reply – *remember what?*

It took another three days for her to respond. Again, it was a simple message. But it spoke volumes. *"I remember Woodenhead. I watched it when I was fourteen."* My message back to her reflected my surprise and elation. *"Really?"*

This time a day went by before she responded. We happened to be online at the same time and were able to have an actual two way conversation.

"I was losing hope of ever finding anyone who remembers!"

"I was thinking the same. But how do I know you're genuine?"

"How do I know you are?"

"Tell me something only someone who's actually seen Woodenhead would know."

"It scared me shitless. Still does. Every single night."

I felt a cold shiver wash over me. But I was still cautious.

"I was hoping for something a bit more specific."

The reply took a moment to come through.

"Just before Gustav nails the piece of wood to Jürgen's head he counts out all little nails onto the kitchen table. It's quite creepy. Is that specific enough?"

I thought about that. It was a detail I couldn't actually recall. But it seemed authentic. I decided to give her the benefit of the doubt.

"You sound like the real deal."

"Thank you. Now you tell me something."

"The theme music,' I typed.

"What about it?"

"Paganini's Sonata number 6."

"Yep. Spot on. I loathe that music. Sometimes I can't get it out of my head."

I could feel the excitement rising within me. Here was someone who had not only seen Woodenhead, but who seemed to have shared similar experiences. I felt the urge to strike while the iron was hot. I typed hurriedly.

"We should meet."

Her reply came back quickly.

"We should."

"How easy is for you to get into London?" I asked.

"London???"

"Where do you live?"

"Inverness."

"Bloody hell! I live in Kent!"

***

In the end we settled for Berwick upon Tweed as a compromise. She came by car. I came by train. I knew what she looked like from her Facebook profile. Narrow face and ruddy complexion, long hair, unashamedly grey, beads twisted into it. A kind of ageing hippy vibe about her. But I was surprised by how tall she was. A whole head and shoulders above me.

She spoke with a gentle highland accent. We spent the day alternating between cafes on the high street and strolling along the old Napoleonic coastal fortifications, struggling to be heard over the blustery wind gusting in from the North Sea.

Appearances aside. it was like meeting another version of myself.

Watching Woodenhead as children had caused irreversible damage to our lives. She had suffered a misdiagnosed mental health assessment, had guzzled prescription medication to the point of addiction and had obsessed endlessly about proving that Woodenhead existed. I could tell from the dark bags under her eyes that she too suffered nightmares and sleep interrupted by terrifying manifestations of Woodenhead.

She'd been an only child and had watched Woodenhead alone. I wondered what that might have been like with no one to argue about it with. Seated at a table with what must have been our fifth pot of tea I showed her Jeff's sketch pad. Her hands trembled as she flipped through the pages.

"And he never admitted to having seen it?" she asked.

"He almost broke my nose the first time I suggested it."

She closed the pad. "And at least he left this as evidence."

I nodded. "And it played its part in us finding each other."

"I have a theory," she said.

28

"Tell me."

She looked at me across the table and held me a moment in a somewhat stern gaze.

"Episode Five," she said.

"It never aired," I replied.

"It did," she insisted.

I gasped.

"It did? You saw it?"

"I am it. We are it. We're Episode Five, Ben. We are how Woodenhead's story continued after he escaped from the robbers."

I paused a moment, letting that thought sink in.

"I've never looked at it that way," I said. "But that kind of makes sense.'

"I have other theories," she said.

There were differences between us after all. I'd spent decades trying to prove something existed. She'd been focusing on why it existed.

"Tell me," I said.

Her answer seemed considerably left field.

"Do you know about angler fish?"

I shrugged. "They have something that dangles from their heads like bait as a lure to draw smaller fish in so they can feed on them."

She nodded. The beaded necklace hung around her neck rattling to the motion. "What if Woodenhead is a lure?" She saw my eyebrows crease. "When he manifests have you ever taken a really close look at him?"

"I'm generally too busy pulling the sheets over my head, or squeezing my eyes shut in the hope that when I open them, he'll be gone."

"I've looked," she said. "It took me a long time to pluck up the courage. But I've looked."

"And?"

"There's something else there, Ben. Something behind Woodenhead's apparition."

"Something else? Like what?"

"I can't explain it. I'm not sure if I can even describe it properly. It's vague and shadowy. It's like the forest in the TV show. Maybe it isn't a forest at all. Maybe it's my mind trying to make sense of what I am seeing. But I'm more and more certain that whatever is behind Woodenhead's supernatural origins is attempting to lure us into the dark space that it occupies."

"For what reason?"

"To feed on us, Ben. To engorge itself on the fear it engenders in us." She chuckled wryly. "The parasite from another dimension. It's sound like a 50's B movie."

For some reason I felt quite angry. Woodhead was easier to cope with if he was inexplicable. Being faced with a possible reason and motivation for his existence set me on edge.

"I think your brother had an inkling," said Morag. "Look at some of his drawings."

I flipped through the pad to the sketch of Woodenhead slashing with the witch's knife. When I looked what I'd assumed to be Matt's attempt at shadowing actually did look a little like an ill-defined depiction of a forest. I glanced at Morag. "But Woodenhead was a TV show. With a plot and actors and all that goes with it. If you look at it that way what you're saying doesn't really add up."

"Think about the lure on an angler fish. It doesn't look like a perfect or in any way exact replica of a fly or a bug. But it's close enough to fool another fish and lure them in. They see something that seems to be a bug and their minds fill the gaps."

"So, we saw something that had the general appearance of a TV show and we filled the gaps with our imaginations?"

She sipped her tea, which by then was probably stone cold. "I think that's exactly how it worked. I think we had to be drawn in close enough that it could gain enough substance to come after us. We were kind of conditioned by the TV shows we'd already watched. I think there may have been others who weren't so easily drawn in. Some fish just swim past the bait and never give it a second glance. Maybe people like us were just somehow attuned to the lure."

"How do you explain the theme music? Sonata number nine exists. We didn't have to fill in the gaps. It was years before I actually found out what it was."

"You're speaking as if I have all the pieces of the jigsaw in place," she said. "I think we both agree that all those years ago something strange and malevolent attached itself to us. To me it makes sense that it has a motive and a goal and is intelligent enough to be able to utilize certain skills in pursuit of that goal."

"Maybe it mimicked the sonata the way a parrot might mimic human speech?"

She raised her teacup. "There you go. Now you have your own theory."

It was starting to make sense to me.

"Episode Five?" I said.

Morag nodded and drained her cup.

***

We parted around seven in the evening. She was going to drive to a cousin of hers who lived outside Edinburgh. My train wasn't till the following morning and I was booked into a little Bed and Breakfast. Her last words before she jumped into her car were. "Don't close your eyes anymore, Ben. Look. See for yourself what's lurking behind."

That night in the B&B I dreamed of the robbers stealing Jürgen away. Lifting the rockers onto their shoulders and carrying him like a prince in his sedan. I heard him scream for his father. I heard the robber's chant that creepy little rhyme.

Hiddle Diddle
Hearts full of joy
Today we have stolen
A wooden headed boy

It bled slowly into Paganini's sonata. Over the mournful drag of the bow across the violin strings I became aware of a rhythmic back and forth creaking of floorboards. My eyes snapped open. Woodenhead had manifested at the foot of the bed, wide grin on his face, hand slashing the witch's knife through the air.

I remembered Morag's words and forced myself to sit up and look. I saw the blood congealed around the little nails that attached the wood to his wounded head. I saw the little nails that attached the ragged flaps of the mouldered flesh from the stumps of his thighs to the seat of the rocker.

He laughed.

He rocked.

He laughed.

He rocked

I didn't look away. I didn't close my eyes. I didn't pull the sheets over my head. I looked and I saw it. The dreadful shadowy place that Morag had observed and Jeff had attempted to sketch. There were truly no adequate words to portray how utterly bleak and alien this place of nightmares appeared now that I was becoming conscious of its existence.

I was gripped in a paralysis of debilitating terror, no longer even vaguely aware of Woodenhead's presence. I saw only this deep obsidian forest. And I knew that somewhere, lurking in its dark lair was the creature which fed on my fears. Drawing it out of me like a poultice draws pus from a boil. I wept and bit so deeply into my knuckles they bled. When it became too much for me, I slumped back and buried my face in the pillow.

Somehow exhaustion must have drawn me into a fitful sleep. I awoke to the sound of crockery being rearranged and the enticing smell of freshly grilled bacon. When I dared to open my eyes a wedge of dazzling sunlight had flooded the room. The vision of Woodenhead and his malevolent puppet master was gone.

Before I boarded my train, I sent a message to Morag.

"I kept my eyes open. I saw. I believe. What next?"

It was three days before I received a reply. What I read chilled me to the bone.

"I'm glad you kept your eyes open, Ben. I'm glad you saw what is really there. As for what happens next, that is entirely down to you. My part in Episode Five is coming to a climax. I'm stepping into that place. That dark forest which hosts the rawest of my fears. I am going to confront the beast and try to end this once and for all. I need you to have the courage to follow me. Become Jack the Giant Killer. Help me to slay the monster."

When we'd parted, she'd pressed a scrap of paper into my hand with her address in Inverness written on it. She'd said it was in case we ever needed to resort to snail mail. I alerted the police. They broke into her flat and found it empty, Paganini's sonata number 9 playing on repeat mode on a little CD player.

Her cousin had not seen her since they parted. She is now officially listed as missing person. I've only known Morag Donaldson for a couple of weeks. I met her only once. But I can't over emphasize the positive impact she's had on my life. I have a purpose now. I am no longer in freefall, attempting to rationalize an elusive phantom.

And I know exactly where she is.

I've come to the conclusion that Morag's Angler Fish theory is, as she suggested, just one piece of a much larger jigsaw. One that may be quite complex. I've been reading up on Neuroparasites. These are parasitic entities that don't just feed on their host; they notch it up a level and manipulate behavioural patterns by somehow by controlling the host's neurological system.

I'm sure that fits somewhere into the bigger picture.

I remain haunted by Woodenhead. He fills my nights and invades my reality.

He laughs.

He rocks.

He laughs.

He rocks.

But I am cognisant of the strange geography of the nightmare monochrome vista that stretches out behind him now. I keep my eyes open. I sit upright. I try my utmost to withhold my fears. To starve the hungry creature which seeks to feed on me.

Eventually I will gather the courage to enter the dark forest that isn't a forest.

Eventually I will find Morag.

Together we slay the beast.

The Death of Each Day's Life
Brooke MacKenzie

The Uber lurched along the dark seaside roads and the copious amounts of rose wine consumed all day sloshed in the stomachs of the three passengers. They had attended the bridal shower of a close friend earlier and were staying on Cape Cod for the night had not been the original plan. The fact is, the wine had been too ample to risk the drive back to Boston.

"This place isn't even rated on TripAdvisor. Are we sure we want to stay here? How awful must it be if no one is even willing to write a review?" Jay whined from the front seat as he scrolled down on phone.

"Well, sweets, it's a summer Saturday on the Cape. This was the best we could find at the last minute." Abby was sitting right behind him. For good measure, she playfully swatted his fedora. Jay clucked his tongue in response and crossed his arms. "I've never been to this part of the Cape before. It's a little more remote, which means that there are fewer tourists than other parts. Plus, there's some great hiking. Maybe tomorrow, if we're not too hung over we can take a hike."

Jay looked around and glared at her. "Sweetie, do you think I brought hiking boots to a bridal shower? I only have my Gucci loafers and the closest to nature they're going to come is the parking lot."

"Well... fine." Abby slumped in her seat and crossed her arms. She wasn't ready to give up just yet. "There's a lot of history in this part of the Cape and the style of architecture dates back –"

"Ugggggghhhhhhnnnnnn..." In the back seat next to Abby, Susan moaned and clutched her stomach. The decadent seafood, pastries and open bar had been too much for her digestive system. She usually ate like a rabbit.

"I hear you, sister!" Jay said from the front. Abby rolled her window down slightly to give Susan some air while trying to scan for familiar landmarks, but the Cape could be disorienting at night.

The Wampanoag Motel was a surprising jolt of light. Its multitude of flaws were accentuated by security spotlights on the exterior and the halo of neon adorning its sign. It was a single-story building with only one other car in the parking lot. *Jay might be right,* Abby thought. The entire thing was either in dire need of a paint job and new roof or full-on demolition, depending upon who you asked. Jay, of course, would have opted for the latter.

"They're going to revoke my interior design license for staying here." He stepped out of the Uber and put his Louis Vuitton mini-duffle—his constant companion—in the crook of his elbow. Susan's torso was still halfway in the Uber as she double-checked for lost items. Abby swatted Jay's fedora again, because it was all she could think to do and gave silent thanks for the spare underwear and mini toothbrush she kept at the bottom of her purse at all times. She had learned to be prepared after a few too many one-night stands. Susan extracted herself from the back seat with a throat lozenge from her pocket and patted the trunk to let the driver know he could leave. The brake lights bathed all three in red for a brief moment.

The screen door to the front office opened with a scolding creak, causing the woman behind the desk to look up from her knitting. She studied the three arrivals over the rim of her bifocals before removing them. "Hi there, folks. I was expecting you two hours ago." Susan and Jay hung back, prompting Abby to take the role of spokesperson for the group.

"Yeah, sorry. There was... wine involved."

The woman behind the desk chuckled and grinned, displaying a mouth like an abandoned building: teeth were missing, broken and graying like neglected windows. The office area was covered in dream catchers of every size and color, causing the friends to weave slightly to avoid hitting them as they approached the desk. There were also carvings of bears, Kokopelli statues and a large drum painted with a hulking figure of a man with deer antlers.

"Wow... you have a lot of Native American art in here. Is it from the Wampanoag? Is that where the motel gets its name?" Abby asked with genuine interest.

The woman, Wanda, according to her nametag—shrugged. "It's a muddy history out here. My grandfather chose the name because there were certainly Wampanoag who lived on the Cape, along with the Sagamore and Mashpee, but who knows if they actually lived in this spot right here. My family owns most of the land on this part of the Cape. Generations ago we were the very first settlers here." Wanda leaned on her elbows and rested her twin gunny sacks of breasts on her forearms. "But as far as I'm concerned, this is all stolen land. The bloodstains might be off the surface, but they run deep underground." She was met with three blank stares. "I'm sorry, listen to me rambling on. Let's get you folks checked in."

Three credit cards were swiped, three signatures scrawled on the black line and three receipts handed back. Wanda picked up plastic motel card keys and held them protectively to her chest. "Before you folks go to your rooms, can I interest you in some dreamcatchers? It gets awful dark and quiet out here at night. Some guests say that the dreamcatchers help put them at ease." Wanda forced herself to keep her smile casual, but she felt desperation squeezing around her voice, raising its pitch slightly. "They really work wonders. They're made by a local guy."

Abby perked up. "Oh, neat! They're beautiful. Is the artist Native American?"

Wanda unhooked a dreamcatcher, an ornate one with feathers and a quartz crystal dangling in the middle and shoved it in Abby's face. "Nope... like I said, it's a muddy history. Not many Native Americans live out here these days. The artist is as white as all of us. Well, not you, of course." She gestured to Jay, who shot her an offended (though not entirely surprised) look. Susan cringed and looked down at her shoes. Abby backed away slowly from the dreamcatcher. Wanda gave her the creeps. "We're all set, thanks," she said, holding out her hand for the keys.

"You're sure now?" Wanda said, turning away protectively for a moment, keeping the keys against her chest, babies nursing from long-empty breasts.

"Yep."

"Suit yourselves. We serve muffins and coffee right here starting at 6:30am." Wanda placed the keys in Abby's hand with a slap. "Sometimes we have fresh doughnuts from the place down the road if the owner over there's in a generous mood and feels like getting up early. Sweet dreams!" Wanda forced a saccharine tone into her voice and once again flashed her broken smile. Abby recoiled a little before managing to smile back.

When Abby, Susan, and Jay were outside they huddled together, afraid Wanda would overhear them. "Guys, seriously, can we inspect the rooms together?" Susan pleaded. "This place is something out of a slasher movie."

"I'm more worried about Wanda," Jay said, gesturing with his head. "There's something off about her."

"You're right about that, Jay. That's one weird woman. What kind of a name is Wanda? And... she could use a dentist." Abby stood between her friends and linked arms with them. "Come on. Let's go look at the rooms and check for monsters under the bed."

They moved as a group to each of the rooms, checking under the beds, behind the shower curtains, inside the cheap armoires and even in the drawers. They double-checked that the deadbolts worked and while the windows couldn't be locked because they all had air conditioning units, the units seemed sturdy enough to make a formidable obstacle for an ax murderer. It was a particularly chilly night during an unusually rainy summer and so there would be no need to use them. When everyone was reassured they would be at least safe for the night, if not exactly spending it in luxury, they retreated to their separate rooms and picked up their communication by group chat.

Jay: Lights on, door bolted, chocolate strawberries that I took from the bridal shower unpacked and ready to be eaten.

Susan: Door bolted, safe and sound. Good night!

Abby: Door bolted! Good night, sleep tight, don't let the bedbugs bite (seriously, this place prob has bedbugs) and don't talk to strangers!

***

Back in the office Wanda swept up the dust bunnies, tucked the signed credit card receipts into the register, and set up the coffeemaker for the next morning. When her chores were done, she poked her head outside and saw the guests were all in their rooms. She clicked the lock on the door and took the drum from the shelf. She tapped it tentatively for a few moments before closing her eyes and letting her hand pound across the taut surface the way her grandfather had taught her as a little girl.

She hummed, wandering in and out of the drum beats. When the song was over, she traced the figure that had been painted in the middle of the drum so many years ago. Body of a man, head of a buck. She put the drum on the shelf and pulled three items out of her pocket: rough bundles of twigs tied into humanoid shapes with red twine. She took a breath and made a rueful cluck with her tongue before setting the figures in front of the drum. "Well, I tried to get them to take precautions, but they're all yours, I guess. Consider the bill paid for one more night." For a second, she thought she heard a scream emanate from far beneath her feet.

***

It took Abby several minutes to get the water temperature in the shower just right, as it seemed to be either freezing or scalding. She squeezed a generous helping of the motel shampoo into her hand. It smelled cloying with a hint of rot, like gardenias just past their prime. There was little difference in size between the washcloths and the towels and the sandpaper texture didn't seem conducive to absorption. After attempting for a few minutes to dry her body, she gave up and wrapped the towel around her head. In the absence of a change of clothes, she put her tank top and underwear back on, inspected the sheets for hair or scabs and jumped into bed while flicking off the bedside lamp in one jerking motion.

Falling asleep had been surprisingly easy—so easy, in fact, that she was completely disoriented when she heard the knock at the door. It took a few groggy breaths to realize that she wasn't back at home in her pristine featherbed and she wasn't dreaming. Another knock came, barely audible this time. And another. And then, a tiny voice on the other side of the door: "Can you help us?"

***

Susan rinsed her face, removed her occasion-appropriate-but-too-easily-wrinkled linen blazer and kicked off her shoes. She pulled the curtains closed and stood at the foot of the bed with her arms outstretched. "Timber!" She toppled forward and landed with a thud, it was harder than she anticipated. "Dear God, if you're out there, please keep me safe from murderers. And please let this night go quickly." She flipped off the light and rolled onto her back. Her tongue was sticking to the roof of her mouth and she debated getting a drink of water from the sink before deciding it wasn't worth the effort. She started counting sheep in an effort to will herself to sleep. Finally, sleep came.

Something stirred under the bed. It was quiet, so quiet, that Susan felt it before she heard it. She pulled the pillow over her head and told herself she was dreaming before chiding herself for drinking all of that wine. *We already checked under the bed, remember?* And the room was quiet and still once again. Her breath deepened and once again she felt herself approaching the precipice of sleep.

Something stirred again. Something that hadn't been there when they checked under the bed earlier.

And then it slid—slowly, excruciatingly—out from its hiding place.

***

Jay congratulated himself as he unpacked his overnight bag and organized his various supplies. Though Susan and Abby had adamantly stated otherwise, he had figured that chances were actually quite slim that any of them would be sober enough to drive back to Boston that night. And so, as always, he came prepared. He had researched better accommodations beforehand, but most places seemed to have a "no refund if cancelled within 24 hours" policy and he wasn't sure he wanted to take that gamble.

Jay dutifully began his nightly winding-down routine, which he had made portable: soothing music on the iPhone, facial exfoliation followed by moisturizing and polishing his Gucci loafers. He lit a cigarette, took exactly five puffs and threw the remainder in the toilet. He brushed and flossed. Finally, he turned on the white noise app, set his phone on the pillow next to him, and pulled on his sleep mask. He was definitely going to leave the lights on.

Sleep overtook him, slowly and sneakily and his breath whistled in his nose. The whistling was soon joined by a rattling sound. And the sound began to multiply.

***

Helping children in need was Abby's entire life's purpose—or so she told everyone. Whilst she loved children, she also knew that she was about two years away from complete and total burnout from her job as a social worker. But still, when a child was in need, it struck an urgent chord in her. When she heard a tiny voice on the other side of the door asking for help, she immediately sat up and threw off the covers. She opened the door and found two kids standing there, wearing identical red hoodies. She couldn't see their faces as their hoods were pulled up and they were backlit by the motel's weak exterior lighting, leaving their faces in darkness. However, judging by their height and scrawny frames, she guessed they couldn't be more than ten or eleven years old.

"Can you help us? We're lost," the one on the left said. His voice—she was guessing it was a boy, but she couldn't really tell—sounded squeaky and sad. "We can't find our parents. Will you let us in?" Abby felt her body rock briefly with an urge to wrap her arms around both of them but her training kicked in. Rule one: do not touch children. Rule two: do not be alone behind closed doors with children. Leave the door open or make sure you have another reliable adult witness.

"Oh dear! Yes, of course I can help you. What are your names?" Abby bent at the waist, resting her hands on her thighs so that her face was at their eye level. The children kept their heads tilted down. Abby waited, but they didn't respond.

"What are your names?" she asked again.

This time the one on the right spoke. His voice was similar to his brother's but had a grittier quality to it. Almost like a growl. "Will you let us in?"

Abby collected her thoughts. "Ok. I understand that you don't want to share your names with me. But I want to let you know that you can trust me. I'm a safe adult; I work with children just like you every day. I'm going to call the front desk and find out what room your parents are in. We will find them together, ok?"

"Will you let us in?"

Abby shuddered, which she registered as a strange reaction. She had cultivated excellent instincts over the years and her judgment about people and situations ran deep within her as an almost primal programming. Something was off here. "I think it's best if you wait outside." They didn't move or respond. Abby started to worry that they were being so protective of their faces, which compelled her to check for bruises. "Please look at me," she said gently. The children didn't move. Abby stood up straight and assumed her best authoritative posture with hands on hips. "Look at me." In unison, the children raised their chins to look up at her. The shadow fell away from their faces. Abby gasped. She had trained herself never to react over the years—she, in fact, prided herself on her impeccable poker face that she presented to children when they showed her their burns and bruises and assorted disfigurements. But this gasp slipped out before she could stop it. The children's eyes were two pairs of pitch-black pools, shimmering terribly, where their irises and pupils should have been.

***

Susan pulled the covers over her head and listened. The floor groaned and creaked as whatever it was that slid out from under the bed unfurled itself.

There's nothing there. There's nothing there. There's nothing there. You just drank too much and got freaked out.

But still the sounds persisted. Tapping. Muffled breathing. Susan screwed her eyes shut and plucked her courage. *OK. On the count of three. One, two, three!* In two sweeping motions, she flung off the covers and flipped on the bedside reading light. And then she screamed.

At first she could only take in a mass of black, but then her eyes focused and her brain slowed just enough to process what was standing in the middle of the room. A tall figure wearing a black waxy robe and mask with glassy eyes and an elongated beak—the kind worn by doctors during the plague. A faint odor of mint and roses wafted from the form—stuffed in the nose of the mask to cover the smell of death—and it tapped its examiner's cane on the floor. Susan scrambled to the foot of the bed, but the sound of a wooden "thwack" was accompanied by a burning pain across her shoulders and she curled up protectively. He had hit her with his cane— the one he used for poking and prodding ailing patients without having to make physical contact.

"OW! Stop! Don't hurt me!"

From behind the mask, a surprisingly high-pitched voice gave its response: *"As I lay me down to sleep, I pray the Lord my soul to keep. If I die before I wake, I pray the Lord my soul to take"*.

Susan tried to get up again to run. This time she was struck across the back three times, emptying her lungs of air, leaving her gasping and flopping like an oxygen deprived fish. He flipped her over and held her down with a gloved hand and, with the other hand he stretched her forearm across a stone bowl and sliced. Her blood made a heavy sound as it hit the bottom of the bowl, the sound drops of blood round and resonant like pennies. A long-forgotten memory from Susan's early nursing classes flared up—primal cures, misunderstood humors, bewildered doctors grasping for mythical cures. He was bloodletting. Draining her of disease. And, as an unfortunate side effect, her life. Susan writhed and fought him, but the wooziness overtook her more quickly than it should have. He bent closer to her, lowering his mask near her face. She could smell the sickly-sweet floral scent and see the glassy eyes flash in the weak lighting, vacant and dark. It was the last thing she saw before she passed out.

***

Jay pulled off his sleep mask and looked around the room. At first he didn't see or hear anything unusual, but his senses began to tingle, so he waited. Then the rattling on the floor started up

48

again. When he looked over the edge of the bed, he saw the carpet seemed to be moving and it took a moment for him to realize it wasn't the carpet. A tangled mass of snakes was wriggling and writhing, a snapping percussion of tongues jutting in and out and a crescendo of hissing battered Jay's frightened ears. He spasmed involuntarily in disgust, releasing a shapeless vocalization. He would have much rather taken his chances with an ax murderer over snakes. He hated snakes.

He jumped to his feet in the middle of the bed, arms spread and knees bent in a defensive stance and surveyed his surroundings for a weapon. *At least snakes don't know how to climb*, he thought to himself. The closest thing he could reach was the Hermes belt that he had neatly rolled into a coil on the nightstand. It was not lost on him that it was a rather snakelike shape. He held the buckle and whipped the belt in the air a few times. *Don't fuck with Indiana Jones.* He almost chuckled when he remembered that Indy also loathed snakes.

He waited, not quite sure what to do next, but he knew there was no way he was setting foot off the bed. The air felt thick with sound and movement and somehow the snakes seemed to be multiplying. He spotted his phone on the nightstand and used it to call Abby. It went straight to voicemail, as did his call to Susan. He grabbed the landline from the nightstand and pressed the number for the front desk. *Come on, Wanda. Pick up. Pick up!*

The ring tone was tinny and far away in his ear, as if the front desk was on another planet entirely.

When he glanced back at the floor, he saw the snakes interlacing like individual muscular fibers twitching in in a monstrous corpus. The phone continued to ring and, as it did, the hissing on the floor began to change and shift.

"What the…" The snakes started weaving themselves together, overlapping their sinewy bodies into a singular, undulating shape. Still, the phone rang. No one answered. He knew that no one would. He kept the phone pressed to his ear—the sound providing a strange sense of security—and gripped the receiver so hard the plastic creaked. The shape on the floor started to grow upward as the snakes oozed in their choreographed formation. As he watched, the snakes wound around each other tightly, precisely, and the individual rattle sounds merged into a singular din. And then, all at once, the rattles stopped. The snakes stopped moving. They had merged completely into one another and formed a figure, solid and unmoving and covered in snakeskin. Jay let the phone drop and a whimper puffed in his throat. The figure was tall, hulking and had the body of a man. On top of its head were two antler shapes.

***

Susan awoke to the sound of the plague doctor speaking in a language that she didn't understand. That high-pitched voice was a grating shock to her nervous system. He had tied a rag around her arm to stop the bleeding, but it felt as if all of her had been completely wrung out. She was too weak to

50

move and her mouth felt doused in glue. She couldn't scream if she wanted to and even if she did she knew it would be futile.

The doctor continued speaking. *"If I die before I wake, I pray the Lord my soul to take."*

He stood over her and removed his mask, replacing the scent of flowers with one she knew all too well. The particular smell of decay that rides in like a trumpeter, announcing death. It's not the smell that accompanies a long-dead body succumbing to rot. It's a more subtle stink and more sickening. The smell of disease consuming organs, muscles and flesh. It was a smell that filled her with a secret terror. She had been in the room with patients who were ripe with that smell and had even held their hands, when what she wanted to do was flail and scream and bolt out the door. It wasn't death that scared her. It was the gray stench of deterioration, of the body wasting away that scared her more than anything. Given her choice of profession, it was a fear that she kept locked away inside.

The doctor's face was decaying. He was bald and his skin was puckered, like it had been in the water for too long and was starting to peel away, beginning at the corners of the mouth. He removed his long black gloves, revealing hands that were covered in weeping pustules, oozing a yellowish, frothy liquid that spilled onto the floor.

Susan knew what he was going to do before he did it, but she thrashed and tried her hardest to summon the strength to fight him, regardless. His wet, diseased hands covered her face. After an endless minute, he slowly started sliding them all over her body, leaving a viscous trail like slug innards. They paused on her breasts, driving home the violating point that he was trying to make. Her body was no longer hers. However, that was not the primary thought that rattled in her mind. She thought of infection and contagion. Illness. Lungs filling with fluid and blood seeping out of orifices. Vomit pouring out of a spasming body. Eyes bulging in breathlessness as organs liquified. She twisted and fought against those hands with the final reserves of energy she had available to her. In the one brief instant that she opened her slime-coated eyes, she could see a dark shape watching from the corner. Tall, broad, with clawed hands reaching over its head. Or were they antlers?

After the doctor had finished running his hands over her, he stopped. She could hear him wheezing—his struggle for breath punctuated by the tell-tale death rattle from deep within the lungs.

"Stop. Just stop. Please." She could taste the glob of infection as it dripped from her upper lip and into her mouth. She began shivering and her body started to ache. Her skin felt paper thin and scalding hot all at once. Her throat seized up and the air became wet in her lungs. Panic throttled her nervous system as a fever started to shut her body down.

"No. Not. Not like this. No…"

She felt the doctor's hand slip into hers, sticky and brittle with sickness. Not at all comforting. It only seemed to drag her faster toward the inevitable, pulling her under as she drowned in her own body.

***

Abby had shut and locked the door, leaving the kids outside and called the front desk three times before giving up. She tried calling and texting Jay and Susan, but didn't get a response from either. The kids had frightened her and admitting this to herself went against everything she had been trained to think as a social worker. But still her gut roiled.

Another knock. "Can you let us in?" Abby stood facing the door with her back against the wall.

"You know what, guys? I can't let you in. But if you go to the front office—"

"But we are lost and scared!"

"Yeah. We need help. Please?"

They knocked again. Harder this time. Abby tried to reason with the more logical and sympathetic part of herself, but something in those primal instincts told her that the kids must not get inside.

"We're just little kids. Why won't you help us?" One of them started to cry. The other one started jiggling the knob—slowly at first and then increasingly faster until the metal started to screech. Abby knew the knob wouldn't hold forever, but the inside deadbolt would keep the door locked.

"Sorry, but you guys need to get away from my door. Now. Please just go to the front office. I can't help you."

The crying one started to sob more loudly. A steady thudding sound came from the other side of the door and Abby realized one of the kids was throwing his body against it. A stifled scream bounced inside of Abby's trachea and her voice came out sounding like it belonged to someone else. "If you don't get away from the door, I'm calling the police!"

The thudding and sobbing stopped. Abby let out a breath.

"But ... how can you do that if the phones don't work?" a voice said, sweetly. Everything in Abby seized and chilled. She did a quick mental check. The room phone and her cell phone had worked just fine only moments ago. She grabbed for her cell phone. The screen was dark. When she tested the room phone, she found that it was also silent. *No.* That word clamored through her bones and body and brain. She had to force herself to keep her thoughts present instead of letting them detach and drift away like they usually did when she was overwhelmed. It was a survival mechanism she had cultivated after years of heart-shredding cases. But she knew it would run counter to her survival in this case. *No. Think, focus and plan.* As long as the cheap motel door held, she would be safe.

The sound was so faint she didn't notice it at first. A squeaking and scratching, like a mouse going about its nocturnal business. That innocuous image gave her some brief comfort, knowing that she wasn't the only living thing in the room. The scratching became more forceful and it took her a moment to process what was happening. The window air conditioning unit was shaking and shifting back and forth on the windowsill. The screws, which had seemed secure during the earlier inspection with Susan and Jay, were actually rusted through and ejected themselves like popcorn. With each jolt, the air conditioner loosened even more and Abby knew that the children with the bizarre black eyes would be crawling through the window in the next few minutes. Her head whipped around, searching. Her adrenaline narrowed her vision to only the essentials. Hiding in the bathroom would only buy her a few extra minutes before they undoubtedly found a way in there as well. But in the bathroom, her eyes settled on something she could use.

The shower curtain was hung on a glorified tension rod with suction cups on either end. Abby locked herself in the bathroom. It took only a few strong pulls for Abby to dislodge the rod. She heard a crash in the other room as the air conditioner fell to the ground, followed by the sound of the children giggling as they clambered through the window. She realized for the first time ever that children's laughter could be a thoroughly menacing sound.

`"Can't you help us?"`

`    "Come out, come out, wherever you are!"`

`   Abby tightened her grip on the shower rod and sucked in her breath. They made quick work of the bathroom lock. The door opened and the two hooded figures stood there, their black eyes utterly absent of any trace of light. Abby finally unlatched her thoughts and let them leave her head entirely. Her body, now ungoverned by her mind, let out a guttural shriek and began swinging. She didn't quite know how it happened exactly, but somehow she found herself running barefoot out of the motel room and into the night, toward a small rectangle of light in a window just down the road.

**

Jay stared at the massive figure in front of him—part man, part beast, created from snakes—and the terror stripped away all parts of him, rather like a snake shedding its skin. He hollered at the top of his lungs and was left with nothing but raw-boned instinct. His gaze scrambled all over the room, wild and seeking. His entire being was comprised of mechanical calculations. Every ounce of energy was devoted to escape. In his impossible, adrenaline-induced clarity he was able to reason that three items on the nightstand would save him: shoe polish, a lighter and cologne. The shoe polish would ignite instantly and a spritz of cologne would turn it into a makeshift fireball. His hands were surprisingly steady, given the fear overdose he was experiencing and he was able to maneuver the lighter and light the shoe polish on his first try. The cologne worked just as he had predicted and he hurled his homemade weapon at the creature. Snakeskin was, apparently, surprisingly flammable, as the creature caught fire right away.

"Motherfucking Maguyver!" The flames spread and Jay leapt from the bed and ran to the door while releasing a screaming flood of expletives.

Somehow he already knew that the door wouldn't open. He jiggled and pulled the knob with everything he had, but it stayed shut. He banged on the door, screaming for help as terror melted his insides and hot tears streamed from his eyes. He heard a crackle and a whoosh and a fiery arm landed across his chest, grabbing him from behind. Everything was a burst of searing heat and Jay released a final scream before the room sizzled into darkness.

***

Abby ran as fast as she possibly could to the house. Someone was surely awake at this late hour and could help her. An alarmed-looking elderly woman in a powder blue bathrobe answered her frantic banging on the door.

"Please! You've got to help me! They're after me!"

The woman's eyes grew wide and she ushered Abby in, bolting the door behind her.

"My dear! You look scared out of your wits! What happened?"

Abby could only hang her mouth open, shaking her head. Words failed her completely.

"Here. Have a seat at the table. I'll get you some tea."

Abby was able to speak after a few minutes. Her voice was thin and shaky. "Do you have a phone I can use?"

"All the phones are down." When she saw the look of horror on Abby's face, the woman rested a hand on her shoulder. "Don't worry, dear. It happens all the time during the summer when the tourists are in town and the power usage is more than these old wires can handle. Here, have some more tea. My cell phone's charging upstairs. I'll get it for you."

The woman refilled Abby's tea and put a plate of ginger snaps on the table before leaving to retrieve her phone. Abby willed her breath to slow and her body to calm. She focused on the repetitive sound of the wall clock. Tick tock, tick tock.

"There's something in the air tonight," the woman said when she returned. "You're the third person to come to me for help at this late hour. I'm so glad I was watching such an interesting TV program that kept me up late." The woman set the phone down in front of Abby and patted her shoulder again.

"I'm the third person?"

"Yes, a pair of boys who were lost came to me earlier—wretched-looking things—and they looked like they had been through the wringer, too. They couldn't get through to their parents, so I gave them a place to stay for the night."

Abby stood up slowly. "Where," her voice caught in her throat, and so she cleared it, "where are they now?

"They're upstairs, sound asleep. Are you all right, dear? You look a little pale. Have a cookie—"

Abby ran from the kitchen to the front door. The black-eyed children were already standing in front of it with their heads bent and hoods forward. Once again in unison, they raised their faces to look at her and Abby turned around to try and find another door. Blocking her way was a hulking, dark figure with a head like a buck. She didn't have time

58

to react. The children had already encircled her with their scrawny arms.

Abby felt a pop in her skull and then her eyes went black.

***

Wanda's alarm went off at 3:00 a.m., just as it did every morning. She put on the same song she always did and sang along to it.

Stars shining bright above you,
Night breezes seem to whisper, "I love you"
Birds singing in the sycamore tree,
Dream a little dream of me.

She did this to inject a little pleasantness into what she knew would be an unpleasant morning. And, since the Wendigo used nightmares as its predatory strategy, she thought of it as a protective balm to sing sweetly about dreams. Not that the Wendigo had any interest in her. She kept him satisfied and well fed. It would be the duty of her family for generations to come to do the same.

She walked from her room to the front office and went through the perfunctory ritual of her morning preparations. She turned on all the lights—including the vacancy sign—and flipped on the coffee maker. She then pulled out the same Tupperware container filled with the same stale pastries that she set out—and brought back in— every day. There would be no one there to eat them.

Say nighty-night and kiss me,
Just hold me tight and tell me you'll miss me....

59

She sang to herself as she snapped on her yellow cleaning gloves and grabbed her bucket. The mess would keep her busy for several hours. It always did.

While I'm alone and blue as can be, dream a little dream of me....

Jay's room was a disaster. The carpet was badly burned and would need to be replaced. Wanda *tsked* and made a note to call the carpet people. She managed to scrub off a dark, pungent substance splattered all over the walls before gathering Jay's things and putting them in his fancy bag. She had no use for any of these things, but she knew her grandfather would be pleased. He always liked it when guests left behind fancy things.

Sweet dreams 'til sunbeams find you,

Sweet dreams that leave all worries behind you...

Susan's room was the least pleasant to clean. A bowl of drying blood stood on the nightstand and there was a liquid mess all over the sheets and blankets. They would have to be thrown out. The room smelled of rotten eggs. Wanda put her hands on her hips before getting to work scrubbing while willing her gag reflex to behave itself. She went about her chores without sympathy or guilt—the same way any innkeeper would when cleaning up after guests of no consequence. She was used to this. It was her duty. But still, singing and humming always helped to make the experience more palatable.

Abby's room was the easiest. The air conditioner unit was banged up and dented but still worked. Wanda would have the handyman out later to reinstall it. There was no trace of mess anywhere, which meant that the girl had managed to escape. Temporarily, at least. Wanda shook her head. "Bless her heart..."

Several hours later, as morning dipped into early afternoon, Wanda had gotten all of the rooms as clean as possible and smelling of sterile lemon. With those tasks finished, she headed back to the front office to make her maintenance phone calls. The Wampanoag Inn would soon be as good as new and ready for a fresh batch of guests. She checked her records from the previous night. Once again, The Wendigo had done his due diligence. There would be no record of the three guests ever staying there. All mention of The Wampanoag Inn on credit cards, in inboxes, on over text message would simply vanish. Any witnesses would have their memories wiped as easily as Wanda had cleared off fingerprint smudges from all of the surfaces. Wherever the search may lead for the missing guests, it would pass by the motel. It always had, and it always would.

She sang to herself as she checked the reservations ledger. *But in your dreams, whatever they be, dream a little dream of me...* Even though she made sure the motel kept a low profile on the Internet—there were only so many rooms she wanted to clean up each day, after all—there were half a dozen guests expected that night. There were always guests and there always would be. After all, the Cape, particularly the area her family owned, was lovely in the summer.

61

DJ vs. the Corona-Dogman
Edward R. Rosick

"You know, maybe we should have been more serious about that social distancing shit," DJ whispered to me as the large, hairy, bipedal thing moved ever closer to us. It was a cold evening in April in the Northern Michigan woods.

While most of the words that came out of DJ's mouth were bullshit, this time I was in full agreement.

***

Our misadventure had begun two days earlier during an afternoon Zoom chat. Me and my Lincoln Park high-school best friends—Hot Rod, DJ, and Weasel—were bored out of our skulls because of the stay-at-home order during the Covid-19 pandemic. We had on-line classes to work on, but we were all seniors and doing homework for classes that we didn't give a damn about seemed like a massive waste of time, bored or not.

"I don't know how much more of this bullshit I can take," DJ said, his words a half-second ahead of the movements of his mouth. He was lying in his bed wearing a faded blue Brawndo! It Makes Plants Grow! Marijuana leaf t-shirt over his skinny chest. "It feels like we've been trapped inside for years."

"It's only been a few weeks. It can't last forever," I said, not truly believing my own words.

"A few weeks is forever when you're stuck in the house with your eight-year old twin brothers and sixteen year old hippie sister, along with a mom and dad who always fight," DJ said.

"I thought your dad hit the road permanently a few months ago. When did he get back?" asked Hot Rod. It looked like he was at his biological father's car repair shop, a rack of wrenches and other equipment behind his brown face, looking just like a younger version of the actor, Wesley Snipes. Not that many people my age would know who the hell Wesley Snipes is.

"He showed up a couple weeks ago," DJ answered. "Said he found Jesus and wanted to come back to save our souls."

"I didn't know Jesus was hiding," Hot Rod said.

DJ ignored him and continued. "After the old man got here, he started on about us going with him to Our Christ the Eternal Truth and Salvation church."

"Isn't that the big mega-church in Riverview?" I said.

"Uh huh. My Mom told him, and I quote, 'no fucking way are we going to a church with a thousand other morons during a pandemic.' Man, they fought about it for days. My old man finally gave up and went to church by himself last Sunday."

"So he's still home?" Hot Rod asked.

DJ shrugged. It was a herky-jerky motion like he was a puppet on strings. "Kinda. He's been banished to the basement."

63

"Why?" I asked.

"Because on Tuesday he started coughing up a storm. You know my sister is a hypochondriac health-nut and the eight year old twins have asthma; Mom didn't want them catching the rona from the old man, so she booted his ass downstairs and locked the door. He was not a happy old man."

"She ever let him come upstairs?" I asked.

"Nope. She throws food down to him every now and then. Says she'll let him up in a couple weeks. Maybe. If he's not coughing anymore."

"DJ"—it was Hot Rod—"where does your dad piss and shit?"

"My mom gave him a couple five-gallon plastic buckets."

Hot Rod smiled. "That was nice of her."

"DJ's mom may be a hard-ass, but at least she's not asking him about his feelings," Weasel said. By the looks of the garden hoses, rakes and long wooden workbench, he was sitting in his man-cave—technically, the corner of their two car garage that he had partitioned off with some old off-white shower curtains. "Last night after her ER shift, my Mom sat me and my three sisters down and made us share our feelings about the pandemic."

"She's probably just worried," I said. "Working as a nurse's aide in the hot-zone at Detroit Receiving hospital, I'm sure she sees some gnarly shit."

"Yeah, cut your mom some slack," DJ said. "She deserves it. Not only is she working on the front lines, she's a milf!"

Weasel frowned and stuck out his long tongue. "That's sick."

"What?" DJ said. "She is."

"That's enough, DJ." It was Hot Rod and the flat tone of his voice meant that if he could have reached through the phone to pop DJ's head off his bony shoulders like a ripe zit, he would have.

"Anyway," Weasel continued, zipping up his tattered black goose-down parka, "between her wanting to know how I feel and my sisters constantly pawing through my room looking for hidden stash, I'm about to lose my mind. You're lucky, E, not having any brothers or sisters to have to deal with."

"I've got you knuckleheads to deal with," I said. "No offense, Hot-Rod."

He laughed, showing off his straight white teeth. "None taken. At least you corrected yourself."

Hot Rod was a great friend, but he also had a helluva temper, one that I had witnessed a few times unleashed on assholes who wanted to make their mark by showing that they were tough guys. After thirty-seconds with Hot Rod, none so far had impressed me as being particularly tough.

"Hey, any of you guys hear about graduation?" Weasel asked.

"Our grades suck," DJ said. "No way we're graduating."

"Fuck you," Hot Rod said. "Me and E are."

DJ shrugged. "Fine. Most of us aren't graduating."

"If we don't, I'm fine with that," Weasel said. "That means we have another year in high school to hang out and get high!"

"Nothing personal, Weasel," said Hot Rod, "but the well with that. If I have to spend one more minute in that old, moldy building, with a punch of stuck-up pricks, then…" he shook his head and reached back into the large styrofoam cooler next to his desk and pulled out a bottle of beer.

"I wish you could pass me one of those," Weasel said. "I'd do anything right now for a cold brew."

"Me too," DJ said. "I'm so bummed that my favorite beer is banned."

"What are you talking about?" I said.

"Corona. You know, where they found the virus."

Now I needed some alcohol. "DJ, they didn't find it in Mexican beer."

"Sure they did. Why do you think they named it the Corona virus?"

"He's got a point, E," Weasel chimed in. "I mean, why name it Corona if it wasn't in the beer?"

"Yeah, I guess you're right," I said.

"Wow, E, you sure gave up easy on that one," Hot Rod said. "You feeling okay?"

The honest answer was no. I was freaked about the pandemic, about graduating, about being cooped up inside and yet not wanting to leave my protective housing bubble.

"I just didn't sleep well last night," I finally answered.

"You never sleep well," Weasel said, "unless you have some good meds to bring on the sandman."

"I know what we all need," DJ said. "We need a road trip."

"Yeah, that would be great," Hot Rod said, "except for that little stay-in-place order from our gov'ner."

DJ waved him off. "Forget that Nazi-stuff. We're Americans—we can go where we please when we please."

"Where we gonna go?" I said. "The whole damn state is on lockdown. There's nothing open."

"We can go up north," DJ said.

"To do what?" Weasel asked.

"We can go look for the Corona-Dogman."

There was silence for a moment until Hot Rod cleared his throat. "The Corona what?"

"The Corona-Dogman." DJ put his hands up, palms out. "Now, just hear me out about this, okay?"

"We're hearing you," I said, not sure I wanted to, but with having nothing else to occupy my bored mind, I figured DJ's rambling could at least kill a few minutes.

"Okay, it goes like this: I was listening to this podcast the other day and—"

"Not another crazy podcast," Weasel said. "I'm a fried pot-head and even I know that most of the stuff you listen to is bullshit."

Since the stay-in-place order, DJ had gotten into podcasts covering everything from hidden Satanic cults in the Vatican to UFO abductees getting anally probed and impregnated in invisible spaceships. And then telling us about it.

"It's not a crazy podcast," DJ said defiantly. "These two guys that were speaking were CIA—or NSA, or DSA, I can't remember—agents and used to work in germ warfare labs all around the world. They said the Chinese military had been using the Yeti—you know, like a Bigfoot, only Chinese—to try and develop germ warfare weapons."

"That's the craziest shit I've ever heard you say," Hot Rod said, "and I've heard you say some pretty crazy shit."

"No, really, think about it," DJ continued, "it makes perfect sense. The Yeti is like a half-man, half-ape monster, right, a missing link. It would be perfect to test things on, since it's like us but not like us."

"I seemed to have missed the part about the Corona Dogman," I said. "Did I have a seizure and miss you talking about that?"

DJ frowned. "No, E, you didn't miss anything, because I haven't gotten there yet. You see, these two guys said that the germ-warfare infected Yeti was what caused the Corona virus to start in China."

"And then what?" Weasel said. "The Yeti swam over to America and started the epidemic here?"

"No, dick-brain," DJ said. "That makes no sense. What happened was that the US Army's secret germ warfare division, along with the CIA— or NSA or DSA— was also testing germ-warfare shit on Bigfoot out west and that's why the first cases of the Corona were in Washington State. You know, where a lot of Bigfoots live."

I took a deep breath and slowly exhaled. "And the way it got from Washington to all across the US is—

"E, sometimes you're not as smart as everyone thinks you are," DJ said. "The Corona is airborne, remember? *Air-borne*. Meaning that sneaky little virus lives and flies in the air. Meaning that it came in the air from Bigfoots coughing and sneezing out west to all other Bigfoots across the nation, as well as to all the people across the nation."

"I didn't know there were Bigfoots in Michigan," Weasel said, the tone of his voice totally serious.

"Sure there are," DJ continued. "Only here we call them Dogman. Look it up on Google. Hell, there's even a great video on YouTube on the Michigan Dogman. Thing is one scary-looking mutherfucker."

"So you want us to go look for this Michigan Bigfoot—I mean Corona Dogman—knowing that it very well may be carrying a deadly virus?" I asked. "Isn't that a little crazy?"

"No, it's not crazy. I mean, we'd all have to wear masks and stuff, but think about it—if we could find proof of this, we'd be famous! And even better, we'd be rich!"

"I'm down to go." It was Hot Rod speaking.

"What did you say?" I was flummoxed. Hot Rod agreeing to one of DJ's crazy ideas was akin to politicians telling the truth—it just never happened.

"You got something better to do?" Hot Rod said before finishing his beer and putting the empty bottle into the cooler. "You gonna start working double shifts at White Castle?"

That was a low blow. I was a cook at a White Castle fast food joint, making hundreds of steamed, onion-soaked burgers a night and hating every minute of it.

"It's slower than hell here at my old man's shop," Hot Rod continued. "The most work I've done all week is change a couple sets of tires for two little old ladies. When I go home, my sister is holed up in her room listening to shitty rap music and my Mom and step-dad are either sitting around bitching about sitting around, or upstairs in their bedroom watching porn and humping the night away."

"What do you say, E?" asked Weasel. "I think it could be fun. Hell, we all get to hang for real— none of this virtual Zoom shit—and go look for Bigfoot."

"Corona-Dogman," DJ corrected him.

"Whatever." Weasel started intently at the screen, his brown eyes magnified by the camera. "E, my Mom just got a new 90-day supply of Xanax. I'm sure she wouldn't miss a few."

He had me. Xannies were my favorite drug in the whole world, slowing down my too-fast brain to almost manageable levels. And with the Covid-19 shitstorm, my anxiety had been upped big time…

"Okay, boys, you've convinced me" I said. "Let's go find us a Corona Dogman."

The next day, we met in the early afternoon (DJ was positive it was best to hunt for the Corona Dogman in the early evening) at Big Joe's Burgers! Voted Biggest 'N' Best Burgers in Michigan! (who voted this illustrious award, I have no idea, since their meat tasted like it was week-old roadkill). While I was happy to get out of the house and see my boys, my hands shook with anxiety. Ten kids from our High School had been hospitalized with Covid-19 and two of them had died. I had been spending way too much time on-line reading every damn theory about the virus and none of it was doing my fragile mental health any good.

Hot-Rod's dark-blue rebuilt 1969 Barracuda sat in the abandoned parking lot of Big Joe's off Fort Street. The day was overcast and a damp forty-one degrees, just another typical early spring day in downriver Detroit. Traffic was non-existent; all the small businesses and shops—more burger joints, pawn shops, bars— were either closed or boarded up, and as far as I could see, we were the only living souls outside.

It almost made me wish for school to re-open.

Almost.

"There's E!" Weasel shouted, pointing at me and bouncing up and down like an excited five-year old on Christmas morning. "We thought you were gonna punk us and not show up."

"And miss all the fun?" I said.

Weasel had on a basic black cloth face mask like me, except his was stenciled with large white teeth holding a fat blunt. He was dressed in Michigan spring-time attire—a thick wool jacket covering a Detroit Lions sweatshirt and baggy blue jeans and combat boots. DJ was dressed in a bulky camo jacket and matching pants, his mask white with a black row of crooked teeth colored in with a magic marker

"Before I forget—" Weasel handed me a baggie with a dozen small white round pills. "Your Xannies."

I dry-swallowed three of them before I opened the door of the car. "Thanks, man. I owe you."

"Plenty." Weasel laughed and pushed up the front seat to get in back. The car was immaculate as always, looking as if it had just come off the line: black vinyl seats shined like a pair of rich trial lawyer's shoes, the dash didn't have a speck of dust and no cans or bottles littered the floor.

DJ followed Weasel into the back; the latter scrunched up against the side like a crab being attacked by seagulls.

"What the hell is wrong with you?" Weasel said to DJ. "You're too damn close! Social distancing, man, social distancing!"

"What do you want me to do?" DJ countered. "Hang out the window?"

"We are not six feet apart," Weasel said, "so you better not have the 'rona."

DJ turned to look at me, winked, then turned back to Weasel and coughed.

"Hot Rod, make him stop pretending he has the 'rona!" Weasel cried. Suddenly his eyes went wide. "You are pretending, right? I mean—"

DJ coughed again, this time louder. I took a step back from the car and put a hand to my face mask.

Hot Rod turned around, scowling. He wasn't wearing a mask. "Cut the shit, DJ. We got a long ride and I'm not in the mood for hearing you two bitch and moan for the next three hours."

"Hot Rod," Weasel said, "I'm noticing here that you're not wearing a mask."

"Very observant. I'm not and I won't. It's all bullshit to me. I mean, how in the hell is a cloth or paper mask gonna stop a tiny virus? It's like putting up a chicken wire fence to stop mosquitoes." He turned to me. "What's your take on all this mask-shit, E?"

I shrugged while keeping my trembling hands in my pockets. "I don't know. I'm not really well-read on viruses." Which was a total lie, but I wasn't about to tell him that.

"And anyway," Hot Rod continued, "this is my car, which means—"

"Your rules," Me, Weasel and DJ all said in unison.

Hot Rod smiled. "Exactly. And one of my rules is that the driver of the sweetest 1969 Barracuda in the United States doesn't have to wear a mask."

"You're always the driver," DJ said.

"DJ, you get smarter every day." Hot Rod adjusted the rear-view mirror so he could look in back. "You really don't have the Corona, right? Because if you do, and you're in my car—"

"I'm fine," DJ said. "I was just fucking with him."

73

Weasel punched DJ in the arm. "Fucker."

Hot Rod patted the front seat. "E, you waiting for an invitation to get your white ass in here?" I always rode shotgun in the 'Cuda because I could and also because I was afraid that if Weasel or DJ did, Hot-Rod would get tired of their incessant jawing and push them out while we were on the freeway.

I smiled, forgetting that no one could see the action under my mask, took a deep breath, then got in and closed the door. The sound of metal on metal caused my racing heart to beat even faster.

Then popped two more Xannies before Hot Rod pulled out of the parking lot.

The desolation outside continued as Hot Rod made his way up Southfield Road to I-75, the highway to all things north. The solitude of the area was creepy as hell: No homeless people pushing shopping carts filled with their only belongings on earth, no kids standing in front of liquor stores hoping to persuade someone to buy them a six-pack, no old men and women walking slowly down the street hand-in-hand, dreaming about the days when they were young and danced and made love all night long. Hell, I didn't even see any stray cats or dogs and the only car we passed was a city cop car, sitting on a side street.

"There's another reason I'm not wearing a mask," Hot-Rod commented. "A young black man wearing a mask driving a sweet-as-hell classic car in the middle of a lock-down order during a pandemic—that would get us pulled over in an instant. The po-pos would have their guns drawn, cocked and locked on my sweet ass before they got out of their ride."

"Can't argue that," I said. "Although my guess is—since it was a city cop—they were having a cup of coffee and watching porn on their phone."

"Maybe, but it just takes one cop having one bad day for a young black man to have an even worse day."

"Hot-Rod, can we stop at A & W?" It was Weasel, tapping on the driver's seat.

"What?"

"The A & W Root Beer stand—it's coming up on the right." He suddenly pointed out the front window, nearly clipping Hot Rods ear in the process. "There it is! There it is!"

"I know where the A & W is," Hot Rod said. "We've only been there a thousand times or so."

"It's closed, Weasel," I said. "All restaurants are closed."

"But I'm hungry," he whined. "And I haven't had one of those sweet root-beer floats in forever."

"I'm sure they'll be open soon," I said, not having any idea if they would ever open again.

"But I wanna go now," Weasel said, his face pressed against the window. "It's not fair."

"The world is having a once-in-a-century pandemic," Hot Rod said. "Nothing about life right now is fair."

"How's your Auntie Charnel doing, Hot Rod?" I asked.

"About the same as she was doing last weekend. Still in the ICU at Outer Drive Hospital, still on a ventilator. The doctor said he thinks she's going to come out of it just fine, but man, seeing her hooked up to a dozen machines, fucking breathing tube down her throat…" he shook his head and said nothing more.

His Auntie had come down with Covid-19 three weeks earlier, one of the first cases in Michigan. I had been over to her house a few times the previous summer with Hot Rod and Aunt Charnel was one of the sweetest people I had ever met. Plus, she made the most dope fried chicken, my favorite food in the whole world. My guilt about not going to see her in the hospital was somewhat assuaged by the fact that they were only letting family members in. When I mentioned this to Hot Rod, he said I could tell them I was his brother.

Which might have worked except for the significance difference in our skin pigmentation.

Hot Rod had the barracuda cruising, one with the road, its radial tires humming their sweet 80 mph sound. The xannies were finally kicking in and I hoped that maybe I could catch a nap, sans dreams of killer viruses. Before I closed my eyes, I noticed that there were no sounds coming from the back seat; both Weasel and DJ were already asleep, the latter's head on the former's shoulder. It was such a cute picture—one that I could use to bust their balls at a later date—that I almost took a photo with my phone, but instead just gazed out the window as we passed over the Rouge River bridge. There were no clouds of dark pollution belching out of the massive smokestacks of the Ford auto plant, no red vaporous glows emanating from the oil refineries and steel plants out on Zug Island. It was like a messed-up surrealistic painting, a post-industrial age purgatory fueled by a world-wide economic shutdown, all caused by an invisible microbe.

Feeling the lips of sleep kiss my anxious brain, I hoped that DJ wasn't finally right with one of his crazy stories. Of course, I forgot that great philosophical axiom: Hope in one hand and shit in the other and see which fills up first.

***

I awoke to the sound that was as natural as springtime rain or a summer thunderstorm: DJ and Weasel arguing .

"Can you guys just shut up?" It was Hot Rod. I opened my eyes and the world had changed from concrete and steel to one filled with barren oak trees and towering pines on either side of us on a narrow asphalt road.

"I would, H-R," said DJ, "but Weasel is just sooo fucking stupid that I can't stay quiet."

I interlaced my fingers behind my fingers and arched my back. "What's the debate about now?"

"'Bout time you woke up," Hot Rod said. "I've been having to deal with these two fools myself for the last twenty minutes and I've just about had it."

"Weasel thinks I'm full of shit about the Corona Dogman," DJ said. "He says—"

"I can talk for myself, thank you very much," Weasel interrupted. "And I didn't say you were full of shit about the Dogman, although you are full of shit about a lot of things. I said that sometimes you tend to exaggerate and maybe this is one of those times."

"Not to bust your ass, DJ, but you're sure the Corona-Dogman is up here?" I said.

DJ shrugged. "I'm not sure-sure, but I'm pretty sure. I mean, the Dogman is super-sneaky. That's why not many people have seen 'em."

"You keep saying Dog-man. You mean there's just one in the whole state?".

DJ shook his head. "You've been eating too many Xannies. Of course there's more than one. I'm just saying they're pretty solitary dudes. We'll be lucky if we spot a glimpse of one."

"You said earlier they'd be up north," Weasel said. "You said, 'there's Dog-men everywhere.'"

"I did not!"

"Did so!"

"Did not!" DJ punched Weasel in the shoulder and he bounced against the side window.

"If one of you breaks anything in my car I'm throwing you both out," Hot Rod snapped. "Without stopping."

"I won't break anything," DJ said, patting the upholstery next to him. "I love this car almost as much as you do."

"Ass-kisser," Weasel said.

DJ filpped him off. "Only if it has a pretty pussy next to it."

"That'll be the day. The only pussy you ever see is your cats."

"Yeah, well, it's not like you're getting any either, my little ugly friend. I know for a fact

Monique is polishing Lamar Hudson's knob and not yours."

Weasel huffed and turned his back to DJ. He was still in mourning over his breakup with Monique Shoniqua Brown, the star of the girl's track team at LP High, as well as the probable Valedictorian. We all knew it was a match that was doomed to failure.

"I told you never to say her name again." Weasel's eyes were wide and dilated and I thought he might began to cry.

"Sorry, man. My bad."

Weasel sulked for a minute more, then turned around and pulled out a dime bag of weed.

"We've been driving forever," he groused while absently rolling a thick blunt. "Why couldn't we go look for the Dogman someplace closer?"

"Because they don't like civilization," DJ answered. "That's why they like it by Mio. That's where a lot of Amish live."

"Amish?"

"Yeah, Amish people. They don't have cars, or phones, or electricity. They live like its 1959 or something. So all their villages are quiet and peaceful and they don't disturb the Corona-Dogman."

"I'm pretty sure most people had phones and electricity in 1959," I said.

"Fine. Then like, 1958. All I'm saying is that the Amish are primitive and so is the Corona-Dogman." DJ smiled and pushed back in his seat. "I've got a good feeling about this trip. And to help out, I brought some special lures."

"Like what?" I asked.

"Can't show you just yet. But it's gonna work like magic."

"Where is this magic gonna take place?" asked Hot Rod. "We're a few miles west of Mio. I doubt your Dogmen are gonna be waltzing down main street."

"Anywhere, man." DJ was looking at the maps app on his phone. "We're now officially in the Huron National Forest, so I'd turn north on any two-track you see that you think the 'Cuda can handle."

"I rebuilt this car from the chassis on up. It can handle anything that I throw at it."

Two miles up a rutted, muddy two-track we were stuck like flies on a trap. After furiously spinning the tires, which only forced us deeper in to the soft earth, Hot-Rod turned off the car. None of said a word as he got out, left the door open and began screaming obscenities at the road, at the mud, at the heavens themselves for cursing him.

"E, pop in the cigarette lighter so I can light this bad-boy up," Weasel said, holding the fat blunt in front of my face. We all knew that being around Hot Rod when he was angry was about as smart as swimming with Great White sharks. Best to just let him vent and get the anger out.

"What are you talking about?" I said. "You know there's no smoking in the 'Cuda."

"But it's some great Jamaican weed," countered Weasel. "I just figured that we'll light up and chill out while we're... you know, not going anywhere right now."

I pushed Weasel's hand holding the joint down. "Listen to me, my friend. You light that up and Hot Rod will fuck you up. Permanently."

"He used to let us smoke in his other car," Weasel said.

"That other car—a '74 mustang two—was a POS," said Hot-Rod, poking his head inside the car. He apparently was done having his argument with God.

"Well, I liked it," DJ said." It had some gnarly wheels. They had like a thousand steel spokes that shined like diamonds."

"It was like trying to pretty up a pig," Hot Rod said. "You can put a slinky dress on a pig, drape it with expensive bling, spray it with sexy perfume, but in the end, all you got is a pig".

Weasel tapped me on the shoulder. "Gimme a Xannie,"

"No. You gave them to me for me. Besides, I only have a few left."

"Shit, man, you need to slow down on those."

"This coming from 'Mr. I smoke a couple dime bags a day of pot'? Yeah, like I'm going to take drug abuse advice from you."

"What's with you, E? Hot Rod asked. "You've been extra-bitchy lately."

What's wrong? You mean besides a global killer pandemic and not knowing what I'm gonna do after I graduate from High School if I live that long?

"E, open your door," DJ said behind me. "Time to make history."

I adjusted my mask before opening the door and getting out, followed by DJ and Weasel. Even with my face mask, the air was different—not laden with the nauseating odors of asphalt and rivers clogged with sewage, but instead fresh, with earthy smells of untilled soil and towering pine trees. With all three of us pushing and Hot Rod behind the wheel, we quickly got the barracuda out of the mud and back onto semi-dry ground.

"You think we're far enough into the woods to find your Dogman?" I asked DJ.

"Yeah, this is perfect," he answered. "And I bet the AuSable River is close, which is good, 'cause the Corona-Dogman needs water."

"All mammals need water," I said.

He pursed his lips. "I know that. I'm just sayin' the Corona-Dogman needs it too."

Hot Rod, who had gotten out of the car, chuckled and opened the hatchback of the car, the interior light illuminating his large camo duffle bag and DJ's backpack. He picked up DJ's pack and went to throw it to him.

"Be careful," DJ anxiously said. "You don't want to break what's in there."

"What have you got that's so special?" I asked.

DJ carefully took the backpack from Hot Rod like it held a gallon of nitroglycerin, placed it on the ground, and pulled out a large pickle jar. Inside were at least a half dozen oblong, 3- inch things sloshing around in thick red liquid. My first thought was that he had brought a jar of bloody cigars.

"What the hell?" Weasel exclaimed. "Damn, dog, those look like—"

DJ opened the jar, and the horrible smell of putrid meat and rotting fish hit me like a two by four. I backed away like a crab trying to avoid a hungry seagull.

"Is that a jar of used tampons?" asked Weasel, covering his mask with his hands. "Have you lost what's left of your stupid mind?"

"Fuck you," DJ said. "And yes, I brought used tampons. They're gonna help us find the Corona-Dogman."

"I told you to stay away from meth," said Hot Rod. "All it does is rot your brain."

DJ frowned. "You know I don't do that nasty shit." He swirled the liquid around and the smell wafted out of the jar. It was like he was fanning a bloated dead horse in the middle of summer.

"Stop!" Weasel said. "You know I got a sensitive stomach."

"Quit being a whiny little bitch," DJ said. "It's all natural."

"So was the big pile of steaming shit my dog dropped on the lawn this morning," Weasel said, "but even that didn't smell as bad as that."

I took another step back. "I know I'm gonna hate myself for asking, DJ, but where did you get those and more importantly, why do you have those?"

"They're my sisters," he answered. "She always has really heavy periods and so, when she threw her rags away, I—"

Hot Rod put out his hand. "Enough. Why do you have those?"

"The Corona-Dogman loves the smell of blood and especially loves the smell of fear-moans, you know, the stuff that drip out of women's pussies to attract men."

"That's pheromones," I said, "and they don't drip—"

DJ waved me off. "I don't stutter. That's what I said—fear-moans."

"Whatever," Hot Rod said. "Just put the damn cover back on that jar and be sure as hell you don't break it."

"Yeah, that would be way nasty," Weasel said.

DJ held out the jar toward Weasel. "Aww, is little Weasel afraid?"

"Get that jar away from me!" Weasel pushed the jar, causing DJ to spill some of the bloody liquid on his own pants.

"Asshole," DJ said.

"DJ, put the damn lid on that jar now," said Hot Rod, the sharp tone of his voice leaving no room for discussion.

"Fine," groused DJ, capping the bloody tampons and placing the jar into his backpack. "But you guys will see—those tampons and their fear-moans are gonna make us rich and famous."

"All they've made you is stinky," Weasel said.

"He's right," said Hot Rod. "Get a bottle of water out of my car and wash those pants off."

While DJ washed the bloody fear-moans off his pants, we went through the gear in Hot Rods duffel: flashlights, glove, and a pair of—

"Are these night vision goggles?" I held up what looked like two small fancy binoculars connected to one another with a metal centerpiece, attached to a thick headband.

Hot Rod smiled. "Pretty bitchin', eh? Borrowed 'em from my uncle;s friend, who just got back from Afghanistan."

"I thought you said you didn't believe in face masks." I held up a black, dual cartridge paint respirator. It looked like half a face from a giant insect.

"I never said I didn't believe." Hot Rod took the mask from me. "I said I didn't believe that cloth and paper masks do a damn bit of good."

I pulled the last piece of gear from a duffel: an eighteen inch long piece of tapered oak that looked like a miniature baseball bat.

Hot Rod took the wood from me and tapping the back tire of his car. "It's my tire thumper. Of course, it can be used to thump other things too."

"You don't need that. I got us covered." We all turned to see DJ holding a snub-nosed Stainless steel .38 special revolver by his side. "If the Corona-Dogman starts anything, I'll cap his ass in a heartbeat."

"Where did you get that?" Hot Rod said.

"I traded some bags of grade-A Dominican weed to Jimmy-D for it last fall, after I got jumped by those four assholes in Ecorse."

DJ, Hot Rod and Weasel had gone to the last away football game in Ecorse last November while I stayed home, sick with strep throat. As Hot Rod told it, DJ had been mouthing off to a group of guys after our football team put a beating on Ecorse. It was one of the more insanely stupid—and

85

downright dangerous—things my intelligence-addled friend had ever done. The four home-boys proceeded to beat the shit out of poor DJ before Hot Rod intervened. The fray cost DJ a broken jaw and two fractured ribs; for Hot Rod, the damage was a handful of skinned knuckles and some serious family issues, since one of the guys doing the beating on DJ, LaMar Means, was Hot Rod's cousin.

Hot Rod held out his hand. "Gimme the gun, DJ."

"Why? I need this, man. Not just for today, but for, you know, when we're out and about. Some of us aren't as bad-ass as you."

"You don't need to carry a piece, man. I took care of you in Ecorse, didn't I?"

"Yeah, but what if you weren't there?"

"What if I wasn't? You gonna start cappin' people? That's a fast way to a life in the joint. You wanna talk to my old man about doing time behind bars?"

DJ's shoulders sagged like a rapidly deflating balloon. He carefully turned the gun around and handed it to Hot Rod, grip first.

Hot Rod opened up the cylinder, then emptied out the five hollow-point rounds and put them in his jacket pocket along with the gun.

"I'll figure out what to do with this thing when we get back home," he said, then looked around. "So we about ready to head out and see if DJ is finally right about something? I mean, it's getting dark."

He was right. The sun was moving low toward the western horizon and would be fully down in no time.

"Yeah, it's almost dark enough," DJ said. "Let's go find us a Corona-Dogman." He made a step into the woods before Hot Rod grabbed his coat.

"No way, stinky," Hot Rod said. "You bring up the rear."

Dejected, DJ pulled on his backpack and brought up the rear of our caravan, with Hot Rod in front, duffel pack over his shoulder, then Weasel, then me. Our walking quickly fell into a practiced rhythm from our times out in the woods hunting and those fond memories, along with the solitude of the forest and the signs of new springtime life—oaks losing their autumn leaves, birch trees sprouting bright green buds—calmed my anxious mind for a rare moment.

When we were at least a mile in the woods, the sun had nearly set, the forest shadows now long and thick. I was wondering how in the hell we would ever see anything in the dark woods when we came upon a roughly circular area the size of half a football field littered with stumps of trees, downed brush, and thorny brambles.

"Logger clearing," pronounced Hot Rod. "Come in, clear cut everything, then move on and cut another section."

"Why do you think they cut here?" Weasel asked, lighting up the fat joint he had rolled earlier in the car.

Hot Rod shrugged. "Maybe there were some kick-ass trees here. Maybe they just wanted to cut shit down. Who knows why? All I know it's a good place to take a break."

"Lemme have a hit of that," DJ said to Weasel, taking the joint and inhaling deeply, then blowing out the smoke in a succession of tight rings.

"Okay, time to lure in a Corona-Dogman," DJ said after two more hits. He pulled the pickle jar out of his backpack along with a pair of thick latex gloves in a plastic bag. "You guys stay here—I'm gonna go in the woods and lay these bad girls down."

"You want one of these?" Hot-Rod said, handing DJ a flashlight.

DJ pushed it away. "Nah. If the Corona-Dogman is out there, the light will scare him off."

"Your choice," Hot Rod said. "But when you trip over a tree root because you can't see it and start screaming bloody murder from your face being split open that will probably scare off the Dogman too."

"I got eyes like a cat and the reflexes of a ninja," DJ boasted. "I'll be fine."

Hot Rod and Weasel finished the joint—I took one hit to be friendly, but weed wasn't really my thing—before sitting down, backs against some large stumps.

"Shouldn't we be hiding?" I said. "I mean, in the one in a billion chance DJ isn't full of shit."

Weasel pointed at Hot Rod. "The Big Guy has night vision goggles. He'll be able to see anything coming at us."

I wasn't comforted by this and voiced my opinion.

"Chill, E," Hot Rod said. "There's plenty of places to hide if I see something suspicious."

"All set," DJ said, coming out of the wood to our left. "Now all we have to do is sit back and get ready to become rich and famous."

Forty-five minutes later—the sun now fully set and the sky partially filled with clouds with a full moon rising on the eastern horizon—Weasel started fidgeting.

"I think you fucked up again," he said to DJ. "I think that this Corona-Dogman shit is just that—*shit*—and we're sitting here in the cold when we could be back home watching movies and getting high."

"Be quiet," DJ hissed. "The Corona-Dogman has really sensitive ears. Your yammer is gonna scare him away."

"There's nothing to scare away," Weasel countered. "The only thing out here in these woods is—"

Hot Rod grabbed Weasels arm. "Shut up. I think I just saw something at eleven o'clock."

"What does he mean, eleven o'clock?" DJ said to me. "I don't think it's that late yet."

I pointed off to the left. "Over there." I tapped Hot Rod's shoulder. "You really see something?"

"Yeah." He adjusted his goggles, then reached into his duffel and pulled out his dual filter paint respirator and put it on before motioning us to get behind a two-foot tall pile of brush and logs.

My heart started racing. Was Hot Rod just fucking with us or had he actually seen something?

"Do you see the Corona-Dogman?" DJ asked over and over like Linus talking about the Great Pumpkin. "Is he out there?"

"I saw something," Hot Rod said, his voice muffled from the respirator. "Something big. And hairy. Walking on two legs."

"It's him!" DJ said. "I knew he was up here! I knew it!"

"Will you shut up?" Hot Rod looked left and right. "Shit. I lost him. Where the hell did he go?"

That question was answered five-seconds later, when, to our left, we all saw it, only twenty feet away.

It was the height of a six-foot man, covered in thick brown fur from its waist to head, the lower body concealed by bushes and the darkness. It moved slowly, pausing frequently to bend down and pick things off of the ground.

"You know, maybe we should have been more serious about that social distancing shit," DJ whispered to me.

"Little late now," I said. "You wanted to find a monster and now we have."

"That's no monster," Hot Rod said, adjusting his night vision goggles once more. He stood up and pointed at the Dogman.

"Hey there!" Hot Rod said loudly. The Dogman turned around, and in the light of the moon peaking through the clouds, I could see Hot Rod was right. It was just a man wearing a thick fur coat. At the sight of Hot Rod, the man screamed and turned around to run, smashing into a large, towering white pine tree. His head hitting it sounded like a coconut being dropped from a tall building onto concrete. The man collapsed on his back, hands out to his side like Jesus on the cross.

I turned on my flashlight and me, Weasel and DJ followed Hot Rod over to the man. "Why did he do that?" Hot Rod asked.

"Your mask and goggles, bro. He probably thought you were a BDSM freak looking for some outdoor action."

"Shit. You're probably right." He took off his gear and I shinned the light on the man.

It was hard to tell his age. His narrow face, with a prominent nose and thin lips, was deeply lined with wrinkles, but his long, unkempt shoulder-length hair was dark brown with only a few smatterings of gray. Underneath the fur coat he had on a tattered *Bernie Sanders for President!* sweatshirt and a pair of torn black jeans.

Hot Rod shook the old man's shoulder. "Hey— wake up."

After a few seconds the man's eyes opened. They were deep blue, like Lake Michigan on a moonlit night. He pushed himself up into a sitting position.

"You them aliens?" he asked in a shaking voice.

"No," I answered. "We're not aliens."

He sighed, a wheezy sound, then chuckled. "That's good. I saw this big ol' U-foe last night and thought to myself, 'self, them aliens finally come back to take you away.'"

"You were abducted?" DJ said with rapt attention.

"Sure was. Back in '99, them little purple buggers—I know everyone says they're gray or green, but let me tell you, they're as purple as the head of a dog's dick—came and got me and took me to their purple ship and did all sorts of nasty stuff." He put one hand over his butt. "Let me tell you—anal probes are no fun at all."

"Why are you walking around in the woods in a fur coat?" Weasel asked.

"'Cause it's cold, that's why." He twirled around like a model on a runway. "Ain't it pretty?"

"Yeah," Hot Rod said. "Very pretty."

"Are you out here to keep away from the virus?" DJ asked.

The man's eyes opened wide. "What virus? Did that new world order finally let a killer virus loose and wipe everybody out? Shit, I knew it! I tol' my ex, I tol' her that the new world order is gonna kill us and we need to live in the woods. But noooo, that nasty bitch called me a crazy old man and left me for some chicken farmer." He looked at DJ. "Can you believe that? A chicken farmer!"

"That's a bummer, man," DJ said, totally sincere in his consolation.

"So are you kids the only ones left in the world?" The old man continued. "If you are, we could all live in my cabin by the river, you know, start over, repopulate the world like Adam and… and…"

"Eve," I said.

"Yeah, her."

"But we're all guys, man," DJ said. "No Eve here."

"Sure there is," the old man said, speaking more quietly now. "I done smelled her."

"What are you talking about?" Hot Rod said.

"Fear-moans, son. Those enticing things women drip out of their who-ha to lure men. Can't you smell 'em?"

DJ turned to me, a look of triumph in his eyes.

"We're all guys here," I said, wishing we were sitting in Weasel's man-cave. Hot-Rod's shop. Anywhere but here. "What you smell are... things DJ threw in the woods to, to—" I glanced at DJ. "You tell him why we're here."

DJ shrugged. "We came up here to find the Corona-Dogman."

The old man gasped. "Why you wanna do that? The Dogman is one ferocious creature! Why, he'll rip your head off and shove it up your ass just as soon as—"

A bone-chilling sound pierced the air, a cross between a howl and a scream. It went on for a good ten seconds and if I hadn't taken a piss before we had started out I would have wet my pants for sure.

"It's the Dogman!" the old man yelled before taking off through the woods like a spooked buck during deer season, swallowed quickly by the darkness.

Hot Rod turned to me. "What was that sound?"

"I don't know. Nothing I've ever heard before."

Weasel turned off his flashlight. "Maybe it was a coyote or wolf, or—"

"It wasn't a coyote or wolf," DJ said. "We've all heard those. It was the Dogman." He pumped his fist up and down in the air. "I was right!"

Hot Rod looked at me. "What do you think?"

"I think we need to find a very place to hunker down and figure this craziness out," I said, before another howl/scream split the night air. That one broke me. I scampered out of the clearing and, in the fleeting light of the moon saw a huge fallen red oak tree to hide under. I dove into the moist detritus under the rotting bark and tried to catch my breath.

"Good spot, E."

I turned around to see DJ next to me. There was no one else.

"Where are Hot Rod and Weasel?" I said, my voice shaking with fear.

DJ looked left and right. "I don't know. I thought they were behind me."

There was a large, tangled collection of brambles growing off the wood. I slowly poked my head up—praying that the Dogman wouldn't rip it off and shove it up my ass—and looked through the tangled canes.

The clearing that we had been in was empty. No Dogman. No Hot Rod or Weasel.

"Do you see anything?" Weasel asked.

"No."

He handed me his flashlight. "Use this to try and signal them. Do three short blinks, then two longer ones, then—"

"I pushed his hand away. "I'm not using your damn flashlight. Didn't you say something earlier about not using flashlights? And besides, don't you think it might give away our hiding place if there really is a Dogman?"

"What do you mean, 'really is a Dogman?' What else could it be howling like that?"

I kept scanning the surrounding area and finally saw my boys. They were to my right at two o'clock about twenty feet away, hiding under some small scrub pines. Still not seeing the Dogman—or whatever the fuck was making that horrific noise—I waved my hand. Weasel immediately waved back and started to stand up before being pulled down by Hot Rod.

"Did you see Hot Rod and numb-nuts?" DJ asked.

"Yeah. They're about twenty feet to our right."

DJ started to move and I stopped him.

"What are you doing?"

"I'm gonna go over to Hot Rod and Weasel. Safety in numbers, right?"

"Yeah, except when there could be a blood-thirsty monster somewhere near."

DJ waved me off. "We haven't heard any howling in like, hours. I bet the Corona-Dogman went after that old man and—"

A string of blood-curdling howls filled the night air and they were close. Damn close. DJ's eyes popped open like a cartoon character and I suppressed a scream.

"It's the Corona-Dogman," DJ silently mouthed.

I numbly nodded in agreement and tried to slow my heart, beating as fast as Alex Van Halen on drums.

There was one more set of howls—this one higher in timbre—then quiet settled in the air like a thick fog. After a couple minutes that felt like hours, DJ poked me in the arm.

"I'm gonna see if I can film him," he mouthed again, pointing at his iPhone.

"No. Stay down."

He frowned. "C'mon, E."

"Stay down," I whispered. "I'll look."

He nodded like a chastised kid but stayed quiet. I strained to hear anything abnormal but there was nothing, just the silence of an evening Michigan forest. No birds chirping, no chipmunks scampering about, no Dogman howling for my blood.

I was so damn scared I had to stop my teeth from chattering. I slowly went from a crouched to a squatting position, rising up just enough so that I could partially see through the brambles in the light of full moon, and immediately wished I hadn't.

The Dogman was at the edge of the clearing, about forty feet away to my right. He was about five feet tall, with a body-builder's torso of wide, muscular shoulders and narrow waist and a very prominent pair of balls hanging between his short legs that ended on small feet. Coarse dark hair covered him from the neck down while his face— like someone had taken a dog and chimpanzee's profile, put it in a genetic blender, then attached it with a stubby neck to the Dogman's body—was covered in finer, light brown hair, like the undercoat on a chocolate Labrador retriever. He was sniffing around some bushes, every now and then raising his head to give another horrifying howl.

I slithered back down next to DJ. "I can't believe I'm saying this, but it's the Dogman."

"I knew it! Now maybe you guys will start to believe me when I tell you things."

The moon hid behind clouds and DJ took the opportunity to sit up and get a look for himself. Thirty-seconds later he dropped back down and clutched my arm like a first date at a horror movie.

"You didn't tell me there was more than one," he said.

"What?"

"The Corona-Dogman. There's another one. I think it's his wife."

I turned toward him, our faces only inches apart. "His wife? What do you mean?"

"I mean there's a second one out there and it has tits."

"This is not good, DJ," I said.

"And I think there's even more," he continued. "I saw some movement in the woods just behind them, but the clouds started breaking and I didn't want them to see me."

"What was the male doing?"

"Sniffing around, although I don't know why— I threw those tampons way far away from us."

"Oh shit. Oh shit!"

DJ squeezed my arm even tighter. "What?"

I pried his fingers off and moved back up. The Dogman—and hell if DJ wasn't right again, because standing at the edge of the woods was another one, just as tall but slimmer in build, with very visible sagging breasts. While the male was busy sniffing around, the female was scanning the perimeter and I froze when I was sure our eyes locked, my anal sphincter tightening enough to crack a walnut. But then she looked behind her. At two more Dog-things. Little dogman-things.

"We're so fucked," I said, crouching back down.

"What now?"

"You're right. There's more. A female and two young ones."

"Like Corona-Dogman puppies?"

"Yes."

DJ grabbed my arm again. "E, this is so great!"

My brow knitted in confusion. "Great? A female protecting her young? Hell, she's the one most likely to kill and eat us."

"No, listen." He pulled out his cellphone. "We can record all of them. It'll be up close and personal. No shaky cam shots, no zooming in from miles away. No one will be able to say it's fake and then we'll be famous and rich."

The male howled again, probably pissed he couldn't find the origin of the fear-moans.

"Listen, DJ, I think I know why the male is sniffing around. I bet he smells the tampon juice you spilled on your pants. You have to take them off and get rid of them now."

His eyes opened wide. "I don't think I can do that."

"What do you mean? You have too."

"I don't have on any underwear."

"You picked today to go free-balling?"

He shrugged. "I forgot to do laundry."

"Look, DJ—you gotta do it. There's no other way."

He sighed. "Fine." With surprising speed and gracefulness he slipped his pants over his boots, rolled them into up and handed them to me.

"Here," he said. "You got a better arm than me. Toss 'em as far as you can."

"Okay." I cocked my arm then stopped. "See if they're looking our way."

He popped his head up like a turtle coming out of its shell. "You're good, man. Throw it."

I threw the pants as far as I could, hoping they wouldn't get hung up on any trees. "What's going on, DJ? Did they go far?"

"Who? The pants or the Corona-Dog people?"

"How 'bout both?"

"The pants went far. The Corona-Dog people are moving off to where the pants landed You know, E, those little Dog-pups are kinda cute. Reminds me of bear cubs I saw at the zoo."

"Yeah, that's great, now listen, when they're totally in the woods, we'll go get Hot Rod and Weasel then—"

My words died in my throat when I heard sneezing. It reminded me of our old cocker spaniel when it stuck its head into a bag of flour.

"What's that?" I said.

"One of the puppies is sneezing," DJ said. "You should see its little ugly face! It's hilarious."

"They got the 'Vid!" It was Weasel's voice, frightened and loud. "They got the Vid!"

"Oh shit! What are the Dog-people doing now?" I asked, trying to not sound as scared as I was.

"They're coming back," DJ said, "looking around for our little stupid freaked-out friend." He slowly brought up his cell phone and I tugged on his jacket.

"Make sure your flash is turned off."

"Of course," he shot back. "What do you think I am, dumb?"

I swallowed my answer and suppressed the urge to take off, to run back to the car as fast as my legs could carry me. Unlike DJ, I had no wish to be famous; rich, sure, but as for famous, no thanks. Being unseen and unknown was much more to my paranoid liking.

"Shit," he grumbled after squatting back down, "I can't get a good shot through the damn brambles and there's not enough light this far away."

"Sorry, man, but at least we're safe and—"

I didn't have time to finish my sentence before DJ suddenly moved from out of our hiding place, crab-walking behind another downed tree, making his way towards the Dog-people.

For a moment I was frozen, my mind blank, wanting to believe with all my cynical heart that this was a crazy dream, a drug-induced nightmare that I would wake up from in my lumpy bed in Lincoln Park and laugh with the boys about it over a case of Strohs, a bag of weed and a handful of Xannies. But the logical part of my brain refused to shut the fuck up, telling me loud and clear that even though it was impossible, I really was out in the woods with a clan of hairy, monstrous beasts.

I slowly moved up again like a whack-a-mole and peered out through the brambles, hoping the Dog-people couldn't hear the frantic beating of my heart, which felt like it was going to crack my sternum any second. They were together at the edge of the clearing, illuminated by the bright moon which had again broken through the clouds. I saw DJ, who was slowly crawling towards them, trying to get the best shot on his camera. Watching him, I sincerely hoped that seeing his bony ass and hairy balls wasn't the last vision I would have of my stoner friend.

DJ went behind another fallen oak. I lost sight of him and it hit me like a two by four between my eyes: I was alone. My heart pounded like I was climbing Everest without oxygen, my breath came in quick short gasps and sweat ran down my sides like I had just gotten out of the shower. I dropped back down, tried to visualize exactly where Hot Rod and Weasel were, and took off.

It probably only took me ten-seconds, but they stretched into forever. I army-crawled through the weeds, sticks and brambles, my hands getting sliced and my face cut, but I didn't care, fearing every second a set of razor-sharp Dogman—or Dogwoman—teeth tearing into my soft flesh.

I heard the click of a hammer being pulled back on a revolver a split second before I saw them and I'm sure a drizzle of piss stained my shorts.

"It's me," I whispered. "Don't shoot!"

Hot Rod carefully released the hammer on the pistol. "I almost shot you, man."

"What are you doing here?" Weasel asked.

I almost broke out into maniacal laughter: *Oh, I'm just crawling around in the forest looking for pixie dust and fairies to show to the nice Dog-people!* "DJ took off and I freaked."

"I hear that," Weasel said.

"Where is DJ?" asked Hot Rod.

"He's determined to get a vid of the creatures," I said. "He's crawling around looking for the perfect place to record."

Hot Rod shook his head. "He's lost what's left of his dumb mind."

"Did you guys throw something in the air?" asked Weasel. "I swear I saw something fly through the air."

"It was DJ's pants."

"His pants?"

"Yeah. I figured that's why the male Dogman was sniffing around—he could smell the tampon juice on DJ so I had him take them off and I threw them into the woods."

"So he's crawling around out there in his underwear?" said Hot Rod.

"He's not wearing underwear."

Hot Rod went to speak, then shook his head and sunk further to the ground, holding onto the gun like a priest clutching a crucifix before an exorcism.

"They're not howling anymore," Weasel said. "You think they're gone?"

"Either that or they're busy eating DJ." I kneeled and looked through the branches. Weasel was partially right; all four of the creatures were making their way slowly back into the thick of the forest, with DJ off to the side and behind them.

"He's gonna get killed," I said, and then, as if DJ was confirming my prophecy, he boldly stepped out into the clearing and brought up his phone to get his elusive footage whether it got him slaughtered our not.

"Holy shit," I said. The moon again broke out of the clouds, illuminating DJ's pale ass as he took another step sideways and tripped over an ankle-high log.

"Shit fuck!" he yelled, arms twirling like a stuntman doing a high-wire act before he fell, slamming the back of his head on another large stump. The Dogman and woman whipped around and started toward the clearing.

"Oh hell." I looked down at Hot Rod. "DJ fell. The Dog-people are coming back. We gotta do something!"

Hot Rod sat up and looked out. He brought the gun up in both hands and leveled it through an opening in our hideout.

Both the Dogman and Dogwoman were now within ten feet of DJ. The Dogman was furiously sniffing the air, spittle dripping out of his ugly mouth, while the Dogwoman was growling like a rabid Doberman.

Weasel popped up next to me to watch the horror show unfold. "They're gonna kill him."

"DJ's not getting killed today," Hot Rod said, but I could uncertainly and fear in his voice and that scared almost as much as the Dog-people.

They were closer now, almost within arm's length of DJ, when Hot Rod pulled the hammer back on the revolver.

"Fuck," he said, voice shaking, along with his hands. "I don't wanna do it, E."

"I know," I said and I did know: sure, we had taken up hunting these past couple years and had bagged ourselves squirrels and rabbits and last year, DJ—of all people—had been the first to nab a ten-point buck during deer season. But all that was different—we hunted for food and our motto, our vow, was 'don't kill what you won't eat.' And as fucked up as we were in every other way, we always, *always* stuck to that motto.

"You gotta take the shot," I said, damn near crying with fear and frustration.

Hot Rod said nothing. He took a deep breath, slowly blew it out and I knew he was going to shoot. Even if he would regret it for the rest of his life, he was going to break our vow and kill for the sake of killing.

And it was at that second when DJ came to.

His brown eyes popped open and a high-pitched scream came out of his mouth as he scampered backward until his back hit another large stump.

"Run, DJ, run!" Weasel screamed. The Dog-people—who had stopped their advance when DJ did his backward crab walk—whipped their heads around, looking for the source of the voice.

Weasel put his hand over his mouth and starred at me. *I'm sorry I yelled but they're gonna eat DJ* I imagined him saying.

DJ tried to stand up but slipped on some wet leaves and fell hard on his ass, legs spayed wide. The Dogman turned toward him again and howled, sounding like a demented wolf on steroids. The Dogwoman, staring at DJ's junk, made a different sound.

A grunting, huffing sound.

Almost like...laughter.

"What the hell?" Hot Rod said, gun still pointed at the two Dog-people. "What is she doing?"

"I know this sounds crazy," I said, "but I think she's laughing."

DJ must have had the same thought, because he pushed himself up with his hands and stood as tall as he could.

"What the fuck are you laughing at?" he said to the Dogwoman. Both the Dogman and Dogwoman stopped their advances and cocked their heads to one side, much like a dog given a complex command.

"I said, what-the-fuck are you laughing at?" DJ said again. "Who the fuck are you, huh?" He pointed at the Dogman. "You ain't got any big junk hanging either, fuck-face!"

Now, I'm sure the creatures didn't understand what DJ was talking about, but they must have picked up on something in the tone DJ's voice. The creatures, along with their little ones standing now next the female, threw their heads back and howled at the full moon, like some special effects werewolf creatures come to life.

This shook DJ; I could see it in his bulging eyes and shaking hands, but he must have reached deep

105

and pulled out a reservoir of courage because he threw both hands in the air like some old-time country preacher and let out a ghastly, ear-splitting scream.

The creatures stepped back, apparently stunned by the audacity and pure insanity of this hairless, half-clothed creature. DJ, his face split with a madman grin, took a step forward. "How do like that, mutherfuckers!" he yelled before throwing his hands up again and again, screaming like a psychotic banshee each time. Walking directly toward them.

All four Dog-creatures scampered back, then turned and ran into the woods. DJ followed them to the edge of the clearing before stopping, apparently figuring that even his dumb luck wasn't limitless.

Hot Rod was out first to DJ, slapping him on the back. "DJ, you'll never be a porn star, but you got some big-ass balls!"

"Yeah, big-ass balls!" Weasel repeated. "I can't believe you."

DJ puffed out his chest. "Yeah, well, fuck those Corona-Dog people. Dissin' on me and laughing like that. I mean, it's not like that bitch's old man was hung with anything special."

"Did you get your video?" I asked.

"Nope. I was waiting for the perfect shot and …well…" he shrugged.

"As my mom would say, what matters is that you're safe," Weasel said. "Although you need to find your pants, man. It's kinda gross seeing your junk hanging out."

"Un uh," Hot Rod said, taking off his mask. "You're not wearing those stinky-ass pants in my car."

"Hot Rod, don't make me sit in the back with him and his junk hanging out!" Weasel cried.

DJ stepped toward Weasel and swung his hips. "What? You also afraid of my big balls?"

"We all need to get our balls and bodies back to the car," I said, looking into the dark woods, "before those dog people decide they're hungry."

"Good point," Hot Rod agreed, picking up his duffel. "Let's go, boys."

"Lemme have your coat to wrap around me," DJ said to Weasel. "Don't want these big balls catching on anything."

"No way. I don't want you nasty junk rubbing on my coat."

I took off my jacket and handed it to DJ. "Here. Use mine. I'll wash it when we get home."

"Thanks, E." DJ pulled up his mask and stuck his tongue out at Weasel. "At least someone appreciates me saving our lives."

The walk back to the car was thankfully non-eventful, with no geriatric lunatics in fur coats or bipedal monsters hindering our journey.

"Why don't you sit in front, DJ?" I said when we got to the car. "A man with stones the size of yours deserves his own seat."

"Really?" DJ looked at me then at Hot Rod, who gave a quick nod. "Thanks! I promise I won't talk the whole time back to Motown and bother you, Hot Rod, because that wouldn't be cool with you letting me ride in the front seat and all and besides, tonight was a pretty bitchin' night, even if I didn't get to film the Corona-Dogman and his bitchy woman and their ugly little dog-kids to make us all rich and famous."

We all got in the car. DJ wrapped his fingers behind his head and sat back in the bucket seat. "Hey E—you think the 'Rona will be gone by the time we get home?"

"Who knows, DJ?" I said before swallowing the last of the Xannies. "Stranger things have happened as we've seen tonight."

"Yeah, you're right," he said. "I just have a good feeling that everything is gonna be back to normal real soon."

I closed my eyes and hoped for sleep. Even though DJ had impossibly been right about the Corona-Dogman, he was wrong now. I didn't know when the pandemic would be over—if ever—and even if it did end, nothing would ever be truly normal again.

Hellen On Earth
R.W. Goldsmith

"I loved him once, I suppose." Hellen gazed at me with half-lidded eyes and arched her back in a languid stretch, coaxing her breasts to peek from beneath the sheets. "Do you think me fickle, Boyd?"

I stood at the edge of the bed and brushed back my hair, flexing just enough muscle to appear unintentional. "Gorgeous as you are, you've every right to be. You deserve better than that toad-faced man you're married to. Hard to imagine what you ever saw in him."

"There was a time when I found Arnold's intellect sexy. He said he'd change the world for me. You've no idea what a turn on it is to have someone promise you something like that when you believe it's possible."

"Arnold works in a cosmetics lab. What was he going to do, change the world with a new line of lipstick?"

"Things aren't always what they seem."

"What's that supposed to mean?"

Hellen swung her legs over the edge of the bed and rose before me. "Nothing. You need to leave. I have to shower before he gets home."

Not talking was fine by me. "Same time tomorrow?"

"We'll see." She pulled me to her and pressed her lips to mine. I reached between her thighs, but she pushed me away. "No. We'll lose track of time."

"So?" I turned her so we faced our reflection in the full-length closet mirror. "Look at us. We're made for each other."

She kissed my hand and, aglow in her nakedness, glided toward the bathroom. "For now. But how do I know it'll last, Boyd? Sooner or later men always disappoint me. Can you promise me you're different? Will you make me happy always?"

"Of course I will, babe. Making women happy is what I do."

"I hope so. I'll text you." She closed the bathroom door behind her.

I awoke at sunup the next day and looked for a text from Hellen. Early as it was, I wasn't surprised to find no word from her as yet. On the other hand, Kat, a tasty barmaid I'd been dallying with, had left me a dozen messages, asking why I didn't reply. Unlike Hellen, Kat was fixated on the most trivial of matters.

After a half-hour on the treadmill, I showered and fixed myself a green smoothie with a heaping side of bacon to fuel the workout I expected Hellen would put me through today. Even endowed with exceptional genes as I was, I'd need to keep in tip-top shape to meet the needs of a woman like Hellen. How she'd ever found satisfaction in the arms of that doughy husband of hers defied explanation.

Hellen had still not texted by ten o'clock. We lived in the same neighborhood, so I considered strolling past her house to see if Arnold's car was there. I'd not yet made up my mind when a pounding came from my front door. From the intensity of the knocks, I thought Arnold had learned of the affair and was here to make a fuss. Jealous husbands were such a bother.

A peek through the foyer window revealed I'd been wrong in my assumption. Arnold wasn't at the door. Kat was. Considering her expression, I'd have preferred an enraged husband.

I opened the door, took in the shapely bare legs extending from Kat's short pink shorts and threw her an innocent smile. "Kat, what a surprise. You should've called. I'm just on my way out."

"You didn't answer my calls. I texted you and everything."

A few houses down the street, a dog yipped without pause, echoing Kat's tone.

I pulled my cell from my pocket and thumped my head. "Dammit, my battery's dead," I lied. "I forgot to charge it."

Kat craned her neck, looking past me into the house. "You're so full of shit. You didn't answer my calls because of Hellen. She's here, isn't she?"

What right did she have to pester me like this? She was no better than that damn dog and its incessant barking. "Why would *she* be here?"

"I was there when you met, remember? You think I didn't see how you two were looking at each other?" Kat stormed past me into the house.

What the hell had I done to deserve Kat's distrust? I'd been so careful to conceal the truth. Leave it to an irrational woman to ruin my perfect morning.

"Boyd!" Dressed in an open silk bathrobe fluttering over a heart-pumping negligee, Hellen raced across my neighbor's lawn.

Much as the sight pleased me, Hellen's timing couldn't have been worse. I'd no time to find Kat and usher her unseen from the house. Through no fault of my own, things were about to get messy.

"Arnold knows," Hellen said, gasping for breath as she reached the stoop.

I pulled my gaze from her heaving breasts and met her icy glare. "What?"

"Did you hear what I said? He knows about us."

"Of course I heard what you said. Why don't you come inside and start from the beginning." Too late, I remembered Kat was inside.

Hellen wrapped her arms around me and pressed her cheek to my chest. "Arnold's done something. I don't know what, but I'm scared."

From behind me came a woman's screech.

I released Hellen and spun around.

Kat glared at me from the end of the foyer. "You fucking prick, I knew it!"

Hellen appeared beside me and wrenched me around so I faced her. She fixed me with her ice-blue eyes and jabbed an accusatory finger at Kat. "What's *she* doing here?"

"She just showed up. I didn't invite her, I swear."

"Oooh, you bastard," Kat howled. "I don't remember you complaining all those times I dropped by after my night shift."

True. But I was in danger of losing both women. I had to salvage what I could. "You have to leave, Kat. It's over. I'm with Hellen now."

Hellen took hold of my hand and clutched it to her breast. I suspected the gesture was intended more for Kat than me. Not that I minded.

Kat fled past Hellen and me and out the door.

The dog's barking turned to a series of distressed yelps before it shut up for good. By the sound of it, the dog's owner had been a bit heavy handed in disciplining the mutt, but at least the barking had stopped.

Kat didn't go to her car as I'd hoped, but ran instead to a row of potted plants that divided my neighbor's yard from mine. From there, she uprooted a shrub with yellow flowers and hurled it my way along with a string of profanity. With that one thrown, she ripped another from its pot and threw it, as she had the first. A few of my neighbors watched from their windows. Some stepped outdoors and looked on from their porches. The Whitmores across the street were out-and-out laughing from the safety of their door stoop. Crap, there was nothing worse than being made the center of a public spectacle.

Hellen tugged at my arm. "She's not important. Arnold's done something. We need to prepare."

"But she's tearing up my yard."

"Then come inside and call the police." She was trying her best to drag me into the house.

"I don't want her arrested. I just want her to..." Several houses away, a black shadow flowed up the street and across the yards. I rubbed my eyes and

113

looked again. Not really a shadow, it was more like countless black ants were speeding my way.

I pulled free of Hellen's grip and pointed. "What the hell is that?"

"Oh God, that has to be what Arnold was talking about. Hurry! Get inside!"

"What are they, insects?"

"I don't know what they are, only that they're bad."

"I don't understand."

"Arnold said I'd love him again when we were the last people on Earth. That's when I ran here. I know him. He meant it literally."

"So I'm supposed to believe your husband's some sort of mad cosmetics scientist?"

"The cosmetics lab is just a front. Arnold heads the genetics division of a black-ops bio-weapons lab. He's been working on some stupid sciencey thing he calls a spontaneous trans-dimensional something or other. Please, we have to get inside."

Somehow I wasn't all that surprised. The day we'd met, not only had the man professed to hate guns, he'd also stated his belief that what our country needed most was a better WMD. Was that what was heading my way?

Fast as cockroaches on rollerblades, the specks surged closer and closer while portions of the advancing tide joined together to form strings of tiny black pearls. They raced towards Kat and the neighbors who stood pointing at the approaching swarm. Despite Hellen's pleading I was transfixed, as were my neighbors. Kat continued with her homicidal cursing and botanical slaughter, apparently oblivious to what was speeding her way. If Hellen were correct, Kat might well be in danger. Despite her irrational behavior, I wished her no harm—admittedly, I was partly to blame for her agitation.

"Kat," I yelled, "get in your car!"

She shook an uprooted chrysanthemum bush at me, flinging dirt from the spidery roots. "Fuck you, Boyd. I don't have to do what you say."

"You don't understand. Look behind you. There's something coming!"

She lowered the plant and turned around. "What…"

"Kat, run," I shouted as a foot-long strand of pearls sped across my lawn.

Kat backpedaled with a shriek. The black strand coiled around her ankle and spiraled up her bare leg, leaving a glistening trail of crimson in its wake. She dropped onto her back on the grass, contorting and clawing at her clothes while shrilling agonized screams. Except for the Whitmores, the neighbors all retreated inside their homes. Several strands reached the Whitmores who collapsed, shrieking and flailing as though lying upon a bed of hot coals.

"Forget her," Hellen cried. "We have to save ourselves."

Kat's pink skirt and blouse dampened with expanding red stains. The string of pearls, now glistening with blood, streaked across her face and through her lush brown hair, fogging the air with a crimson mist. The strand, grown three, four times as long as before, zoomed down and around her neck, then vanished beneath her blouse once more. Like a racing chainsaw, the strand ripped trenches in her flesh, devouring her alive.

Kat's screams weakened. Two strands streaked around her thighs, another gouged furrows across her cheeks and nose. The damned things were multiplying as they butchered my once attractive lover.

Hellen gave my arm a forceful tug. "Forget her. I need you. Come inside, or I'll lock you out."

Kat ceased her screaming. Her body shrank before my eyes. More and more of the black strands zipped around her body. One of her legs, now little more than bone, separated at the knee and rolled free.

Hellen released my arm and fled inside the house. I followed her and slammed the door.

I pushed Hellen toward the upper-floor staircase. "My room's upstairs on the left. Go. I'll be there in a sec."

Not waiting for her to comply, I ran to the kitchen and grabbed a claw hammer from its home in the junk drawer. I wasn't sure what good the hammer would do against such a threat, but any weapon was better than none.

Then I hurried to the washroom, held two bath towels under the shower and splashed my face. The shock of the chill water washed away all hope that this was a dream.

I returned to the front door, set the hammer on a console table and stuffed a soggy towel along the doorsill. With the space beneath the door sealed, I did the same to the back door and rushed upstairs to my bedroom. I doubted the towels would do any good, but it was the only idea I had.

Hellen stood staring out the window. Gunshots rang out from up the street. Screams issued from nearby homes. The crunch of a car crash sounded in the distance. The steady blare of a horn followed.

A shattering of glass came from downstairs. So much for my efforts to keep the damned things out. Windows were no obstacles to the creatures. In addition, I'd left the hammer on the console.

I squeezed beside Hellen at the window and gasped at the shroud of black specks swarming the neighborhood below. Everywhere I looked, the blackness sped about, overrunning the yards and street, winding their way over trees, fences, walls and rooftops. Oddly enough, this window was about the only thing not covered by the things.

"There're ten-times as many as there were a minute ago," Hellen said. "They just keep multiplying."

"We only have to hold out till the military comes." I made myself sound more optimistic than I was. To contain these creatures, the military would need to incinerate the area to the extent that nothing survived, including the both of us. Fast as their numbers were growing, I suspected they reproduced by dividing themselves like the flatworms I'd dissected in school. If that were the case, the infestation would never end as long as a single pearl survived.

"They're everywhere," she said. "They're pouring into the rain gutters, into the sewers. They're spreading everywhere. What good's the army? They might as well try and rid the world of flies and my husband's too smart to have made his creations susceptible to bug spray."

I turned on the bedroom TV. I didn't have to switch channels to find what I sought. Video news footage jumped from one city to another. In each, tiny black pearls swarmed as they did outside my window. Below each scene, a different name flashed: London—Paris—Moscow--Tokyo—Beijing—New York. "My God, how could it have spread so fast? Your husband must have planned this for months, maybe years. This couldn't be about you and me. It was only yesterday we first made love."

Hellen looked away and threw herself on the bed. "It's complicated."

"Complicated how?"

"I don't know. It's not my fault. I don't like to think about it."

"What's not your fault?"

"I get bored, okay? I didn't know he'd do something like this."

"What's boredom got to do with anything?"

Hellen's eyes moistened. "Don't yell at me. It was hardly anything at all."

"For God's sake, Hellen, what did you do?"

"Nothing, really. It's just that you're not the first, okay?"

I felt like I'd taken a steel-toed boot to the balls and I scrambled to interpret her meaning with something other than what I knew she meant. I came up short. "How many men *have* you screwed around on your husband with?"

"I told you I was fickle. Isn't that enough? You shouldn't try and make me feel bad."

"Dammit, Hellen, he's destroying the world because of you!"

"It's not my fault he's jealous. What was I supposed to do, stay home and do nothing?"

"Doing nothing's a far cry from screwing every man in town."

"It wasn't *every* man and I've changed. From now on there's only you. I swear."

"Easy to say when we're about to die."

Hellen spread open her robe, parted her thigh, and slid her hands down the slope of her belly. "Make love to me, Boyd. Show me you still love me."

After everything she'd confessed, how could she think I still loved her? And why the hell was I was so fucking aroused? But hell, odds were I'd soon be dead. Why not get some while I could?

I pulled off my shirt and threw it across the floor. If this were to be my last time, I might as well make it good, no matter how much her wantonness tore at my heart.

She reached out, grasping to draw me in. Her succulent lips blossomed with a sweltering smile of lust. But there was something false about her smile that gave me pause. Much as I ached to fill her, I wouldn't be manipulated.

I raised my hands and backed from the bed. "No. This is all a game to you. I'm not playing anymore."

"You're wrong. This isn't a game. How can you not believe me? I love you."

119

"I thought I loved you too, but now I'm not sure. I'm feeling kind of used."

"But you have to love me! I'll die if you don't." Hellen pulled her robe around her and pushed from the bed toward the door.

"Hellen, no! They could be out there."

"I don't care. Life's not worth living without you."

"I know, babe, I know, I'm not saying we can't work things out, but we can't if we're dead."

I turned to face a sound like tinkling raindrops coming from behind me. On the outside of the window, a single black strand skittered about like a yard-long centipede. I grit my teeth as I crept closer for a better view. Three rows of crescent-shaped legs extended along the underside of each pearl, propelling the glossy black orbs over the glass with a sound like sprinkling rain. Tiny black spheres with legs, that was all there was to them, not even a mouth. How they consumed their victims was beyond my comprehension.

Two more strands scuttled onto the window. I called out to Hellen. "Come here and check this out."

Hellen looked at me and shrugged. I stepped clear of the window for her to see. She shrieked like a rat had run up her leg. I suppose I should have warned her first.

She spun around, yanked open the door and screamed again. At the end of the hall by the staircase, the walls, floor and ceiling were black with pearls. She slammed the door and catapulted herself over the bed and into my arms. "They're everywhere. We can't get out."

I glanced at the window. The pearls were no longer there. But why? Glass was no deterrent to the creatures. Crazy as it was, I could think of only one explanation.

I stepped back from Hellen and tapped the glass. "What do you see?"

"Nothing."

"Exactly. The creatures aren't on the glass anymore. Help me test something, will you?"

She gave me a suspicious look, then nodded.

"I only need you to wait here while I go to the door."

"You won't leave me?"

"No. Never." If I were correct, leaving her would not be an option.

I released her hand, hurried around the bed and put my ear to the door. I heard through the wood what sounded like the patter of rain. I beckoned Hellen. "Come here."

With hesitant steps, she walked my way. The rain receded to silence. At the window, the panes darkened with pearls.

I wrapped my arm around her shoulders and pulled her close. "We're going to be all right."

I reached for the doorknob.

She pulled at my arm. "We can't go out there."

"Trust me," I said and turned the knob. I prayed I was right.

With a deep intake of breath, I pulled open the door. As before, the creatures amassed at the end of the hallway. For a dozen feet beyond the door, the hall was clear. I emptied my lungs with a sigh. "It's you, Hellen. You're keeping them away. Your husband must have done something—I don't know what—but something to keep you safe. We're free to go where we want as long as we stick together."

Hellen took a furtive step into the hall. The creatures retreated an equal distance.

She turned and gazed into my eyes. "They really won't hurt me?"

"I don't believe so, no."

"Then I want to go home. My bed is so much nicer than yours."

Was she seriously proposing we go to her house for the purpose of having sex? Could she not grasp the whole end-of-the-world concept? "We need to find your husband. See if he has a way to stop these things."

"No. I hate him. I'll never forgive him."

"We have to try."

"He'll make this my fault."

"All you did was fall in love with me. How could anyone blame you for that?"

"He will. He can be so... so self-centered. I'm going home. You can look for him if you want."

"You know I can't do that. Not without you."

"Is that so bad? What more do we need when we have each other?" She pressed against me and ran her hand through the hair of my bare chest. "What do you say, once we're home, we get out of these clothes so you can slip into something more comfortable?"

I nearly dragged her back to my bed. Only the sound of rainfall coming from the stairwell brought me back to my senses. "Damn it, Hellen, I'm serious. We need to find your husband. He might be able to stop this."

"But all he'll do is lecture me on what it means to be a good wife. You don't know how dreary he can be with his incessant blah-blah this and blah-blah that. From the way he goes on, you'd think I'd never slept with him. Well, I did. But no more. I'm done with him. He's a liar. He isn't changing the world for me. He's changing it to upset me. I'll never forgive him. Never."

Hellen pushed away from me and walked toward the stairs. "I'm going home. Arnold had better not be there. Are you coming?"

The black pearls receded before us as we descended the stairs. The towels lay shredded across the floor. As Hellen drew near, the last of the creatures streamed outside beneath the door and through a broken window to the side. She picked up the hammer I'd left on the console and dropped it into the pocket of her robe.

Outside, a half-circle of exposed front yard extended twelve feet or so from Hellen. Beyond the clearing, the world was awash in black pearls, so dense as to muddy our surroundings in a roiling gray haze and though the sky was a cloudless blue, the world was awash with the sound of rain.

With stiff steps, Hellen led us down the walkway. The clearing surrounded us in a near perfect circle. She neither paused nor looked Kat's way as the receding black tide laid bare the polished bones. I, myself, being a sensitive man, suffered a genuine moment of loss before looking away.

We came to the street and Hellen turned toward her home. "Shit! I knew it was too good to last."

I followed her gaze, certain my doom was near. At the end of the street, a vertical black form emerged from the speckled landscape. Whatever it was, it was coming our way. "What is that?"

"Guess." Hellen resumed walking toward the shape.

The shape took on the bloated form of a man immersed in a coat of black pearls. The figure walking toward us was the only man on Earth with the wherewithal to survive beneath such a blanket of death, Hellen's cuckold husband, Arnold. Though I wanted to stomp the man's head into the pavement, I vowed to restrain myself and do whatever was necessary—short of sacrificing my self-respect—to learn of a way to end this nightmare, for, were I to save the world, untold fame would be mine. I'd be the world's savior, the celebrity of the year, an acknowledgement I humbly deserved.

Arnold approached and passed through the perimeter of Hellen's pearl-free space, his wriggling black coat stripping away like grime squeegeed from glass. Though the creatures left him alive, he'd not come away unscathed. A profusion of scratches bloodied his pudgy hands and face. He was dressed in the frayed remnants of a white lab coat and dark slacks. He smiled sheepishly at Helen.

In response, Helen cursed him under her breath.

We came to within six feet of each other and stopped.

Arnold pulled a handkerchief from his hip pocket and dabbed blood from his eyes. "Hello, dear."

"Don't 'dear' me, you selfish prick. Look what you've done."

"Yes, they're far more effective than even I predicted."

"You've ruined everything. Who's going to do my nails? I hate you."

"It doesn't have to be this way, Hellen. Not everyone has to die. I can stop it. All you have to do is come home and be a proper wife."

There it was, Arnold had admitted he could end the plague of black pearls. If I failed to convince him, trick him, or force him into revealing the means, Hellen would have to submit to his demands so I could save the world.

She rolled her head and turned to me. "Here we go again. What'd I tell you? He's obsessed with our stupid vows. He's so demanding. But you're not like that, are you, Boyd? You'll never tell me how to behave. You'll tell me how beautiful I am and make love to me day and night and always make me happy, won't you?"

My response stuck in my throat. For some reason, this didn't quite sound to me like the paradise she envisioned. Sure, sex with Hellen was better than great, but there were other things in life beyond sex, such as sports and weekend barbecues with the guys and action movies and hanging out at clubs, not to mention all the late-night talk shows I'd be on if I saved the world.

I placed a finger to Hellen's lips so I might speak, and turned to Arnold. "How does she know you're telling the truth? About you having a way to reverse this, that is."

"Do you think it's a coincidence that both Hellen and I are free to walk about while you'd be reduced to bones were you to leave her side? A simple compound in her morning coffee has rendered her repellent to my creations."

Arnold paused to wipe blood from the bridge of his nose. "Unfortunately, the formula doesn't affect men the same as it does women. I can tell you first hand, the appendages of those little devils are sharp, though, as you can see, the injuries are only superficial. Be that as it may, the chemicals for the compound are readily available. It requires only a modicum of intelligence to prepare, though it might prove difficult for you, Boyd. I can post the formula online for those who are still alive."

He turned to Hellen. "What do you say, dear? Come home and be mine as you were meant to be. I'll even immunize Boyd. Of course, that's on the condition you never see each other again."

Arnold patted the blood from his mouth. "So what's it to be, dear? Shall we consummate the deal with a kiss?" He then closed his eyes and puckered his lips.

Hellen said nothing, narrowing her gaze in thought.

Whichever decision she made, I'd be the one who lost. If she accepted Arnold's proposition, I'd lose Hellen forever. If she chose me instead, the world would never know the hero I might have

126

been. Being the selfless man I am, I did what I had to do. "Kiss him, Hellen. You have no choice."

Hellen turned to me and then back to Arnold. With a scream of rage, she wrenched the hammer from her robe and, with a swung of her arm, buried the claw in her husband's bald pate. Arnold dropped where he stood, wrenching the weapon from her grip with his weight.

Eyes blazing, she turned and shoved me away. "Fuck you, Boyd. You're lucky I don't bean you too. Who are you to tell me I have no choice? There's always a choice. Didn't anyone ever teach you that? God knows there's nothing worse than having someone tell me I have no choice."

Her features softened. She took my hands in hers and kissed them both. "I'm sorry. It's Arnold I'm angry with, not you. I don't want to ever be angry with you. I only want you to make me happy."

I pulled my hands from Hellen's and knelt beside Arnold. He lay with his cheek plastered to the pavement. Fresh blood mingled with the drool trickling from the corner of his open mouth. Pupils wide and fixed, he stared past the hammer's wood handle with a cockeyed gaze. I felt for a pulse.

"He's alive." It was all that could be said for the man.

Hellen reached down, took my hand and beckoned me back to my feet. "He's not important. I'm with you now."

"We can't just leave him like this."

"Of course we can. There's no one left but you and me. We can do whatever we like. You still love me, don't you, Boyd? Tell me you love me."

I'd no place to go, no place to hide. Black pearls darkened everything around us, pattering with their ceaseless sound of rain. But for the sky and Hellen's twenty-four-foot-diameter haven, the world belonged to Arnold's monstrosities. So numerous had they grown, tree limbs sagged beneath their weight. So dense had they grown, they dripped from the power lines like hot tar. With nowhere to land, not even the birds were safe.

"Of course I love you, Hellen." What choice did I have? "There's no one else but you."

Even if she weren't crazy-ass sexy, gorgeous and smoking hot in bed, she'd soon be one of the last women on Earth. So sure, I loved her in a self-preservation sort of way and I'd do whatever it took to keep her happy. Even so, I knew my days were numbered. Tragic as my situation was, my awesomeness would not save me from Hellen's true nature. There'd be others who survived. There always were. And no matter how hard I worked to satisfy her, the time would come when she'd tire even of me.

Hellen truly was a fickle woman.

The Ghost of Christmas Past
Dorothy Davies

Susanna stood in the sharp clear December sunlight flooding the empty bedroom. 'This is mine!' she thought with a surge of excitement. 'Mine! Bigger than my other one! I'm going to love it here! I want my bed over there...'

Her thoughts stopped abruptly as she saw a young girl standing by the door. She was wearing a pretty blue dress, black patent shoes with white socks and a big smile. A mass of blonde ringlets framed her innocent looking face. There were blue ribbons in her hair.

"Who are you?"

"Who are you?"

It was simultaneous. Susanna and the girl began to giggle behind clenched fists as they stared at one another, then the laughter broke out and they were speechless for a few moments until it subsided. Then they stared at one another again.

"I'm Susanna."

"Hello Susanna, I'm Harriet." She walked into the room, smiling and looking round her.

"I thought everyone had left." Susanna was wondering why Harriet was in the empty house and whether she should tell Mummy or Daddy there was still someone here. She hadn't been forgotten, had she?

"Are you part of the family that's moving in?"

"Yes. Mummy and Daddy and Buster and me."

129

"Who's Buster?"

"My rabbit. He'll be here tomorrow. He's a house rabbit, he lives indoors."

"I always wanted a rabbit; no one let me have one, though."

"That's a shame. I love Buster."

She looked round. "This room is so pretty with its blue wallpaper and carpet."

"It's my favourite colour. I asked for it all to be blue."

"It's my favourite too!"

"Susanna, who are you talking to up there?" her mother called from the foot of the stairs.

Susanna was about to answer when she realized Harriet had a finger to her lips and was mouthing *say nothing.*

She shouted, "No one, Mummy!"

"I should hope not. Come and help me unpack!"

"Got to go. I'll be back," Susanna reluctantly walked out of the bedroom and down the stairs.

The removal men were working hard and her father was trying to help by carrying boxes. Susanna got a big smile as she moved out of their way and went into the lounge, a room she liked. Its pale rose patterned paper and soft pinky coloured carpet appealed to her. She didn't know why, but it did. The TV, chairs and sofa had already been put in place and a load of boxes had been stacked in the middle. They were marked with huge labels, LOUNGE, BEDROOM, SUSANNA'S TOYS. Susanna pulled open th'e box of toys and began taking them out.

130

"Not in here, silly!" Her mother came in looking flustered and tired and began to put them back. "When the men get your furniture upstairs, you can unpack the box. There's nowhere to put them otherwise, is there?"

Susanna was disappointed; she wanted to find a doll to give to her new friend, the one she couldn't talk about. Harriet was a secret. Susanna could keep secrets.

She already had one big one to keep.

"Come and help me put things away in the kitchen." Susanna obediently followed her mother, itching to get back upstairs and talk with Harriet, to find out why she was still there.

The box marked KITCHEN was in the middle of the black and white tiled floor. "Let's get everything out, shall we? Then we can decide where it all goes. We ought to make everyone a cup of tea." Her mother was her usual bossy self but something was different, not quite right. Susanna couldn't work out what it was. That made two puzzles for her to think about. She decided Mummy was stressed from the move, all that work, all that packing up and unpacking. It had to be that. One puzzle solved. Harriet was the other and she wasn't so easily solved, because she couldn't ask an adult about her.

Everything came out of its wrapping paper and left on the familiar kitchen table, ready to be put into unfamiliar cupboards and drawers. Susanna kept thinking about Harriet. Where had she come from? Why was she still here? Would she like a doll? Where were her toys and clothes? Where did she sleep? Who had been feeding her while the house was empty? Why had she stayed here? What about Christmas presents for her? How could she find something to give her that wasn't old?

"You're very quiet," her mother commented as she put saucepans in a cupboard, making a lot of noise with them. "Don't you like the house?"

"Yes, it's nice. When are we going to put the Christmas…"

There was a bang and a shout from the hall and her mother rushed out to see what had happened. Susanna opened a drawer out of interest and found a child's spoon with an animal head engraved in the handle. She put it in her pocket, thinking she would give it back to Harriet next time she went upstairs. Then she wondered how she knew it belonged to her.

Where did Harriet sleep? There were three bedrooms, one for Mummy and Daddy, one for her and one… that had to be the room where Harriet lived. She would go and explore later.

"Nothing to worry about." Her mother bustled back into the kitchen and went on unpacking. "Won't be long before they start taking the beds upstairs." She stopped and looked closely at Susanna. "Are you all right, sweet one? You look a bit-"

"Yes, Mummy."

"You do like your room, don't you? I think we chose the best one for you."

"Yes, it's nice. Can I say where I want everything?"

"Of course you can! Why don't you go upstairs now? They'll be bringing your things up soon."

"Ok."

Susanna hurried back up the stairs, hoping to see Harriet again, to tell her about the spoon, but her room was empty. She opened the door to the room next to hers and looked in, thinking she would be in there, but it was empty and dusty, unloved, she thought, and wondered why.

"Where you want your bed, kiddo?"

The removal men were on the landing with her furniture. They had called her kiddo from the moment they'd arrived. She smiled every time, especially at the older man who was a bit like her much loved Granddad. She hurried back into her bedroom.

"Over there, please, by the wall."

"Good place for it." The bed was put down gently, as if it was made of china. "Gonna get some more of your things."

She walked over to the windowsill and looked out. The garden was big, it had trees and bushes and would be good to play come summer. Right now the trees had no leaves left and the flower beds looked empty, so what had made the flash of blue she had seen? She shivered, wondering when Daddy was going to turn on the heating. When the men had done, she thought, they've got the door wide open. But I'm cold. I need a sweater or something.

Why hadn't the girl been wearing a sweater or jacket? The dress, that pretty blue one, had short sleeves and yet she hadn't looked cold.

"Box of books, Susie." Daddy was looking tired and flustered now, like Mummy. This moving thing was hard on grown-ups.

"Thanks, Daddy. I'll put them on the shelves when the bookcase comes up."

"And here it is!" The Granddad removal man had it in his arms. "Over here all right?"

"Yes."

"Yes."

Susanna almost gasped when she heard the voice but stopped herself in time. There were two grown-ups in the room and she knew they were not to know about Harriet, not yet anyway, not until she knew what this was all about.

Dressing table, wardrobe, stool, boxes of clothes, everything she possessed was in her room. Someone had thought to bring the box of toys up from the lounge, too. Daddy smiled at her as he went out, then held his head for a moment as if he had a bad headache. She wanted to go to him but he was hurrying down the stairs.

"Let him go."

"I wondered where you'd gone."

"Out of everyone's way. They can't see me like you but they can bump into me and that hurts!"

"You're not real, then?"

"No, of course I'm not! Oh I see, you thought I got left behind! No, this is my home."

"I wasn't sure if you were real or not. I wanted to give you a doll."

"That's really nice of you, Susanna but I'm a ghost; I couldn't hold a doll. Really, you are kind. No one has offered that before."

134

"A ghost! Really?"

"Really."

It needed thinking about. Susanna began unpacking the box of toys, sitting the dolls around the wall. It was a start, it made the room more her own. She could see Harriet reaching out and then not quite touching them. *A ghost,* she thought. *A ghost in my room. I wonder if Mummy and Daddy can see her, too?*

"Susanna, come and have some tea!"

"I've got to go," she told Harriet.

"Yes, I know. I'll come with you but ignore me. Don't let them know I'm here. They won't like it; they might get someone to send me away. You need a friend, Susanna."

It was strange eating tea in a new home: everything was unreal, different; the light in the kitchen, the layout of the cupboards, Daddy's weary smile and the gruff voices of the removal men as they stood in the hall drinking tea. Seeing Harriet standing by the cooker made it even stranger, it was all Susanna could do to concentrate on what she was eating and drinking and not keep looking at her new friend.

You need a friend, Susanna.

It was as if Harriet had looked into her head and seen her loneliness. She had looked forward to the move: their old house had been small and dark, this one had space and light, but it had meant moving to a new area, a new school, leaving her friends and familiar things back there, back where familiarity held her firmly in its arms.

You need a friend, Susanna.

Yes, she did, someone to talk to about why Mummy preferred the too-smiley 'Uncle Ralph' to her quiet, solid, friendly Daddy. Mummy didn't realise but she knew when they 'went to their room' – to kiss? What else they did she didn't know but once upon a time Mummy and Daddy had come down smiling and cuddling. Now they came down like two separate people. She remembered the time she came home from school earlier than usual and found Mummy coming down from her room with 'Uncle Ralph'. She looked - sparkly. She wasn't sure they'd been holding hands, but...

That was the time 'Uncle Ralph' had given her a £2 coin and told her not to tell her daddy he had been there. She had taken the money with a 'thank you' but no smile and put it in a box. She didn't want it mixed up with her other money, without knowing why. Because it came from him? The question was too big for her to answer.

That was her big secret, one she found it hard to keep locked inside. Now she had two secrets, but if she could talk about one of them with Harriet...

Who was a ghost.

A real ghost.

Not something out of a storybook.

A girl who could – as she just did – disappear in a blink.

And reappear outside the window in the garden.

"Did I see someone outside then?" Mummy was staring out of the kitchen window, looking very puzzled.

Daddy looked round and smiled. "You're tired, Emma. There's no one out there. Buster will be, tomorrow."

"Buster doesn't look like a person, Eddie!"

They laughed and the moment went away. Susanna released the breath she didn't realize she was holding until that moment. Inside she was shaking, whether with laughter or fear Harriet would be caught out, she didn't know.

"I'd better get Susanna's curtains up and her bed made." Mummy walked to the door. "Coming, Susanna?"

"Yes."

She hurried up the stairs after her mother, half waiting for the hint of blue, but nothing happened.

It didn't take long for her bedroom to look pretty, long blue curtains to match the bluebells in the wallpaper and a surprise, a new duvet set, also in blue, so her whole room matched. She was pleased.

"There you go, honeybunch. All done. Now for our room."

"Mummy, who's going in the other room?"

"Which one?"

"Next door to me."

For a moment Mummy looked almost secretive, but then said, "no one at the moment. It's our guest bedroom if anyone wants to stay over. We have to get it kitted out. All right?"

"Yes, thank you."

"You OK to put your books on the shelves?"

"I can do that."

137

"All right, I'll make a start on our bedroom, then."

Harriet appeared the moment the door closed. *"You got something that makes a noise, Susanna?"*

"Yes, why?"

"We don't want your mother to know I'm here with you if you speak aloud. Put something on, make a noise."

"All right." Her radio was on the bookcase; she switched it on and began sorting books.

"That's good." Harriet sat cross-legged next to Susanna. *"She's having a baby! That's who's going in that room!"*

"A baby?" At first Susanna felt a thrill of happiness and then a terrible stab of jealousy. She was their baby, their child, their much loved daughter, or so they had always told her. She slotted books on the shelves, banging them against the back. The news was unwelcome.

"Are you sure?"

"Of course I am! I've seen enough to know!"

"Oh." So that was why they moved, that was why there was a 'guest bedroom' waiting for furniture. That was why Mummy had been going to the doctor's all the time… it made sense.

"How does it feel?"

"What?"

"To think you'll have a brother or a sister."

"I don't know – yet. I have to think." In fact, her mind was in a whirl. Baby clothes, milk, squalling in the middle of the night… why did her parents put her in the room next to them when they knew a baby was coming? Or did they?

She put a handful of books on the shelf and looked at Harriet. "Do they know?"

"No. But they will, very soon. Your mother is sure but she hasn't told anyone yet."

"Can you read minds?"

"Sort of."

"I don't like it."

"That's what I thought you'd say."

"Time for bed, Susanna!" Daddy was calling from outside the door. Harriet disappeared as swiftly as she came.

"All right, Daddy! Come and see my room."

He came in, radiating smiles, warmth and security. "Looks good, little one, it really does. Pretty colours."

"I'm a bit tired."

"Course you are, sweetheart. It's been a long day. You warm enough? I turned the heating on as soon as the men left."

"Yes, it's warm in here. Daddy, when will we put the Christmas tree up? And can we have the wreath on the door like always and put the cards up like always? And can I hang my stocking over the fireplace?"

"Everything will be like always, honey, just in a different place, that's all."

"When do I have to go to school?"

"So many questions! Ask Mummy, she's got it all written down. Not yet, though, you've got time to get used to being here and making new friends."

Susanna risked a glance at the doorway, but Harriet was nowhere to be seen.

"All right, I'll get ready. Will you come and kiss me goodnight?"

"That's one question I can answer, of course I will!"

The bathroom was bigger than the old one, the mirror was a little bit higher and Susanna found she couldn't see herself as she cleaned her teeth. Everything was strange, more than she expected it to be, as if she had to grow into the house in some way. There was plenty of room to grow – if no new arrival came along. In that moment she knew she didn't want a brother or a sister to disrupt her life. She would be much happier if the other bedroom was really for guests, not for a baby. She hurried and got into her bed. At least that was familiar, even if the room wasn't. Her nightlight cast a gentle glow on the blue carpet and walls.

'I could really be happy here,' she thought, 'if I didn't have to worry about a baby and the secrets. I wonder if 'Uncle Ralph' will visit Mummy? Hope not.'

After her daddy had been to say goodnight, Harriet came soundlessly into the room.

"Go to sleep, Susanna. All will be well. I know what you want and what you need. I will see to it."

"Thank you," Susanna murmured. As she slid into a deep sleep she wondered what Harriet was talking about.

***

There were Christmas cards hanging from cords stretched around the room and a towering tree

140

standing on a small table in the window, flashing lights glittering on the baubles, ornaments and angels hanging from the branches. It was a new tree, to celebrate the first Christmas in their new home, Mummy said. Susanna liked it but mourned the loss of the old one, the familiar tree with its half bare branches from so much use. That was more Christmassy to her, the old; the loved. This would be all right, in time this would be Christmassy too, but right now it wasn't.

New or not, it gave her that funny tummy feeling of excitement. Christmas was coming and in that other empty, unloved bedroom was a big pile of boxes covered with a dust sheet. She knew they were presents and longed to lift one corner and see what was there. She didn't dare, it would spoil Christmas morning if she did.

She could ask Harriet but it wasn't possible for her to lift anything, or so she said.

Harriet had promised her an early Christmas present. Susanna had no idea what it would be. What could a ghost possibly give her?

She told Harriet she didn't need a gift, it was enough for her to have a best friend to talk with, someone to confide in about her hatred of the too-smiley Uncle and her doubts about his friendship with Mummy. He was the only person Daddy didn't know anything about and that worried her.

"Don't worry about him, he's gone," Harriet told her one night. *"Gone out of your life. Wasn't hard to do. That's my present to you, Susanna, one of them, anyway."*

141

Susanna didn't ask what Harriet meant. She didn't want to ask; she had a bad feeling and was afraid to talk about it. Harriet didn't seem to want to pursue it, either, she talked endlessly about the Christmas tree, the decorations, the many cards, all of which seemed to surprise and entertain her.

Three days before Christmas Susanna was sitting in her room with the door wide open when she heard Mummy on the phone with her sister.

"You remember Ralph, Lou? The guy I worked with... he was killed in a car crash last week. I just found out today. It was in the paper."

Susanna crept to the banisters and pressed her face against the railings, trying to hear what was being said. "Supposed to have swerved because of a little girl in the road. Hit a tree, it said. No girl was seen, though, by anyone." She paused for a moment. "Yes, bit of a shock. Well, that's in the past now, that job and everyone who was there. I just have to forget it." Then they went on to other things, the house, the amount of lovely cards they had, plans for the garden come Spring.

Harriet was standing on the top stair, hands on her hips, head on one side, looking at Susanna.

"Told you!" She seemed to be gloating. *"Told you I'd see to it!"*

Susanna walked back into her room and sat on the bed. "Dead?"

Harriet sat cross-legged on the carpet. *"Dead as I am."*

"You don't seem dead to me."

142

"I don't feel dead, but when I do this-" one hand went right through the frill on the duvet, *"I know I am."*

"What if he comes here, dead as he is?"

"He won't. He doesn't belong here. I do, so I'm here."

Dead. Was Mummy sad? She didn't sound sad but then, she was talking on the phone and she wouldn't give herself away to someone by crying. They would want to know why.

She looked at Harriet. "Dead and gone?"

"Dead and gone."

It was like a black cloud lifting from Susanna's mind, one she hadn't realised was there. No more creeping around the house – not that he had been to this new one – no more wondering why Mummy thought he was nice.

She smiled. "Thank you!"

"You're a good friend, Susanna. I will do anything for you."

"Will you come to school with me when I go in the New Year?"

"Oh, now you're asking! School! Yuk! Yes, I will, but not to learn anything. I did that years ago and said I never would again! I will come so I can tell you who to be friends with and who is not a real friend."

Susanna thought about that. It would be a great help, sometimes she made friends with someone and told them secrets, only to have them break friends with her and blab her secrets half round the school. Yes, she decided, that would be good. As long as no one could see Harriet.

143

"Don't worry, they won't see me!"

Susanna smiled again. Another worry, one she didn't realize she was worrying about, had been lifted from her mind.

"I wish I had black hair like yours, Susanna."

"I like your blonde curls."

"Perhaps we could swap some time; that would fool them, wouldn't it?"

Susanna laughed. "We couldn't do that!"

"We can do anything, you and I."

Susanna frowned. That sounded almost ominous. She thought about Uncle Ralph, swerving to avoid a little girl...

"That was you, wasn't it?"

"What was?"

"You made Uncle Ralph swerve and hit the tree."

"Yes. How else was I supposed to kill him for you?"

Susanna went cold. *How else was I supposed to kill him for you?* She had only wanted him to stop visiting. But perhaps there was no other way to stop him visiting. A ghost would know that, she wouldn't.

"I didn't want... mean... was that the only way to stop him?"

"Susanna, trust me. I know what I'm doing. He was coming here right after Christmas, when your daddy was away on some – contract, he calls it, doesn't he?"

Susanna nodded.

"I heard them talking. I had to stop him, didn't I?"

"Yes, but – dead?"

Harriet started laughing. *"That's as definite as it gets, Susanna. Never again to come into your life. You didn't know, did you, he was looking at you like a grown man shouldn't."*

"How…"

"You haven't asked me once how I died, have you?"

"No, I…"

"I fell down the stairs. I fell because I was running away from a man who looked at me like that Ralph looked at you. Only this one had done a lot more than look. He had – touched me where he shouldn't… lots of times. I had to get away from him. I fell and broke my neck."

Tears filled Susanna's eyes. "You were…"

She couldn't find the words. It was something she couldn't imagine, but then memories of the too-smiley man crept into her mind and she knew Harriet was right about 'Uncle Ralph.'.

"There's one more gift to come, Susanna."

"You don't have to…"

"Yes I do. You've been good to me. You're the only one who has spoken to me, the only one who offered me a doll, the only one who gives me your time. I love you, Susanna. You're the sister I never had."

"I love you too, Harriet." She wondered, in her secret heart, if Mummy had a little girl, would it be the same. Then she thought about it for a few minutes. She was ten. The baby would be – a baby. They would not be proper sisters for – a long, long time.

Then there is no point, she thought, surprising herself with her adult attitude.

***

Christmas Eve finally arrived. To Susanna it had seemed like eternity but it was here at last. The TV was on, Buster was asleep in front of the fire; Daddy had been drinking whiskey and looked happy and content. Mummy looked tired and worried. Harriet explored the Christmas tree for what must be the thousandth time and Susanna just wanted to get this last sleep done so she could have her presents.

The lounge looked cosy; its pink walls and carpet giving it a warm feel that went to her heart. The Christmas cards and decorations made her heart turn over with excitement and anticipation. In that moment she was bursting with happiness, thinking life could not get any better.

"I thought we would do something different tonight." Daddy sat up and reached for a thin book with a worn cover. "Turn the TV off, Emma. I thought we would read A Christmas Carol tonight."

Mummy looked up and grimaced. "Do we have to? I hate ghost stories."

"I thought it would be good to start a new tradition here in our new home. It isn't that scary."

"No, I hate ghost stories, really, Dan. I can't…" She got up and left the room, all but banging the door as she left. Her father looked at Susanna. "Do you want to hear the story, honeybunch?"

"Yes, please, Daddy!"

146

Harriet came to sit on the floor at Susanna's side.

"A story!"

"Yes."

The book was already on the table. Susanna could hear her mother clattering dishes in the sink in the kitchen, determined not to hear a word. She wondered what it was that her mother was really afraid of, or was it that with Harriet's presence she had no fear of ghosts?

Her father began reading and Susanna became absorbed in the story, almost forgetting Harriet sitting by her side until she whispered:

"That's me, the ghost of Christmas Past."

Susanna didn't answer her. The story ended, with its lovely warm-feeling happy ending. During that time Buster had gone to his bed, her mother had stopped making a noise and had actually crept back into the room when all the ghostly parts had been read out. She sat down in her chair with a silly apologetic smile.

"Did you like the story, honeybunch?"

"It was good, Daddy!"

Then the bombshell exploded. Her mother leaned forward, still with that silly smile, and said:

"This time next year we will be a family of four, Susanna. We might even have our own Tiny Tim. Are you pleased to be having a sister or brother?"

Susanna sat, shocked and speechless. Harriet had been right. That was who the empty room was for.

"Told you!"

147

Her father laughed. "You've shocked the child, Emma! She doesn't know what to think!"

Susanna tried to smile. Then, remembering her manners and wishing to avoid answering the question, said "Thank you for reading the story, Daddy. I really liked it."

"Good." He stretched and yawned. "I guess we all ought to get to bed, then. Christmas is coming!"

When she was in bed, Susanna began turning over thoughts in her mind. The story had affected her on different levels, the ghosts of the different Christmasses coming into her mind. She remembered the comment from Harriet, *that's me, the ghost of Christmas past.*

"Harriet," she whispered. "When did you die?"

"Christmas Day. Go to sleep, Susanna! It will soon be time for presents and fun and perhaps my last gift for you."

Susanna lay still, thinking of Harriet dying on Christmas Day as she tried to escape someone who wanted to hurt her. She was aware of tears as she slid into sleep.

***

Harriet woke her early next morning by impatiently hissing in her ear: "W*ake up! Santa's been! There's presents under the tree and things in your stocking!"*

Susanna scrambled out of bed, wrapped her robe around her and hurried downstairs. When she got downstairs she looked at the clock: 7.15. Not

148

too early, if she was quiet, she wouldn't wake anyone anyway.

The tree lights had been left on overnight, they shone on the wrapping paper and bows of the many boxes. *"Open something!"* Harriet was as excited as Susanna, who was trembling with anticipation.

In a remarkably short time she was surrounded by presents: books, clothes, shoes, pretty jewellery, a host of beautiful and interesting gifts. Harriet was exclaiming over everything without once looking sad or jealous that she couldn't touch any of it.

The door opened and her parents came in. "You got down here early!" her mother said with a smile that turned to a grimace. She held her stomach as if she was in pain.

"I got here at-" Susanna looked at the clock, "7.15. Now look, it's just 8 o'clock." She was proud of her ability to tell the time so precisely.

"That's not too early, honeybunch."

"Something wrong with your mother, Susanna?"

"What did you do?"

"Nothing ... yet."

Her father was gathering up the wrapping paper. "Looks like Santa was good to you," he commented, with a sideways glance. Susanna went along with the joke.

"He found out where I had moved to. Clever, isn't he?"

Her mother laughed, then turned to go to the kitchen. "You'll want breakfast; I'll go get it started."

149

Susanna watched her go, saw how she was stooped over, not walking upright as she usually did. "Daddy, is Mummy all right?"

"Well, the baby is giving her a few problems. Nothing for you to worry about, if it gets any worse we'll call the doctor."

"Or an ambulance," Harriet whispered.

"Do you think you ought to get dressed before breakfast, honeybunch?"

"Yes, I'll get dressed now, Daddy."

"Do you need any help?"

"No, I can manage. I'm big enough, thank you."

"Wear the new red velvet, Susanna."

"Why?"

"For a reason."

"All right."

She picked the new red dress up from the floor and took it upstairs to her bedroom. It fitted perfectly and went well with her dark hair. She looked at herself for a few moments in the mirror, then went back down for breakfast.

"My, you look good!" her mother said when she walked in. "I liked that dress when I first saw it; I knew it would be good for you."

"Thank you, Mummy, Daddy, for everything."

"Don't thank us, Santa Claus bought it!"

"Daddy, Mummy just said she knew the dress was for me when she saw it! Santa wouldn't know what size dress to get me!"

"You caught out!"

They laughed and for a moment they were joined together as a family. For a moment Harriet

150

was not included and Susanna caught a sour look on her face. Then it went and Harriet laughed and ran out of the room.

Susanna's mother looked round. "Do you know, Dan, I swear this house is haunted! I keep catching sight of someone, a small someone, in blue."

"Pregnant women have all sorts of strange things happen to them, Emma. Don't worry about it."

"I'm not worrying, Dan, just don't like it, that's all."

"We don't have a ghost here, Emma!"

Don't we?

Susanna went back to the lounge and picked up some of her presents to take to her room. She wanted some of it out of the way before Buster came romping in to play.

Harriet went with her as she climbed the stairs.

"You've got some nice things, Susanna."

"Yes, I wish I could share them with you."

"I can look, even if I can't touch."

"Is that enough?"

"It has to be, it's all I can do."

"Mummy's coming upstairs."

"Shall we play a trick on her?"

"What sort of trick?"

"Remember what I said about changing places?"

"Can we?"

"Yes, like this."

Susanna looked in the mirror and almost shrieked. It was her face but it was surrounded by

151

blonde curls and her red velvet dress had become a pale blue one.

"Quick, go out on the landing!" Harriet was all but pushing her.

Susanna walked out of her bedroom just as her mother reached the top of the stairs. She took one look at Susanna, screamed and fell all the way to the bottom.

Her father rushed out of the kitchen to see what had happened. By then Susanna had gone back into her room, looked in the mirror and saw she was herself again, with black hair and red velvet dress.

"What did you DO!" She spun round to confront Harriet.

"Gave you your other gift, Susanna. There will be no baby now - or ever."

Susanna heard her father frantically phoning 999 and asking for an ambulance. There was a sick feeling in her stomach. She went to the banister railings and looked down. Her mother was lying very still and there was blood coming from her head – and her body. *That was my fault. Mummy's hurt and it was my fault.* She began to cry, but whether it was for her mother or the thought Harriet had died just that way she didn't know. The sick feeling had been replaced by a cold empty core that made her shiver. Tears poured down her face and she began to sob.

"Susanna!" her father called. "Get your coat and shoes on! We have to go to hospital with Mummy! I can't leave you here on your own!"

"All right, Daddy!" Susanna ran to get her shoes and then hurried downstairs, stepping over her mother who was moaning softly, saying something about seeing a ghost. *Shut up, Mummy,* she thought. *Don't tell anyone, they'll think you're mad.* She frantically mopped at her tears, which didn't want to stop.

She got her coat and put it on. The siren was approaching fast. Her father was crouched by her mother's side and taking no notice of her.

"Open the door, Susanna, please."

"Yes, Daddy."

There was a flurry of activity as the paramedics tried to stop the bleeding, then hoisted her mother onto the trolley and rushed her out to the ambulance.

"Come on, Susanna!" Her father swept her up into his arms. That at least stopped the tears.

"Stay here, Harriet!"

"I will! I'll take good care of our home, Susanna!"

"Will..."

"Yes, she'll be fine. I promise. Now you're safe. You are the only one and will stay that way."

Susanna sat in the ambulance watching one paramedic working on her mother and another one taking details from her father.

No baby.

No squalling brat in the empty bedroom.

No other person to take her parents' attention and love away from her.

It was as if a huge weight had been taken from her, she felt so much lighter. Even her mother's serious condition didn't dent the new feeling she was experiencing.

Her father looked across at her and tried to smile. "Everything's going to be all right, honeybunch. Don't worry."

"Yes, Daddy."

Of course it is. I have all I want. You and Mummy to myself and a best friend to give me whatever I want. Watch out, school...

The ghost of Christmas Past had become the ghost of Christmas Present and given her a very special gift, one she would never forget – or regret.

Until The Light Takes Us
Paul Edwards

Part I

"Cam, listen.

"I've moved to a higher plateau. I'm beyond flesh now.

"One person, one person alone means nothing. We can *change, really we can, but we have to evolve and expand.*

"Cam... listen. I've seen another world.

"Let me take you."

July, 1994

The man parked his Escort in a layby, then killed the engine.

Sunflowers rustled. Birds shrilled. A dead yew raised twisted arms to the sky, as if in praise of the encroaching night.

He stared into the rear-view mirror, contemplating the three little girls in the back. Their wide eyes shimmered with worry, fear and confusion. He felt for them. Wanted so badly to save them.

Too late.

He opened the car door.

"Daddy?"

"Shush," he whispered.

He closed the car door, then approached the chapel by the side of the road. He went inside, swiftly disappearing into thick, dust-choked darkness.

For a while, there was silence; it was as though the world was holding its breath. Finally he re-emerged, looking dazed and confused, his eyes shining in the dreamy, purplish twilight.

He returned to the car, opened up the back-passenger door. Knelt down and faced the first little girl.

In her eyes he saw his own face shimmer, tremble and shine.

"You have to do something for me." He gripped the girl's hand, smoothing it, squeezing it. "I want you to go in that chapel." He looked at the other girls. "All of you. One at a time."

The first little girl began to cry. "I don't want to, Daddy."

"You must." He lifted her from the car. "It's for your own good."

The first girl walked uncertainly away, glancing fretfully over her shoulder as she advanced, the chapel looming over her like a silent bird of doom.

May, 2014

In the dark of their flat, Megan and Cameron watched the late evening news together. It was filled with the usual stories of death, misery and despair.

A couple had blown themselves up in a restaurant in Djibouti. Boko Haram had pillaged three villages in Borno State, killing twenty-eight people and kidnapping many more. Ten people had been killed in an attack by al-Shabab on the parliament building in Somalia. Twenty-seven dead following an overnight raid on Yemeni government buildings in Seiyun.

"Christ," Cameron whispered, shaking his head from side to side.

"What?" Megan looked up and around, eyebrows raised, face pale in the darkness.

"The world's gone crazy. How can people claiming to be human beings murder people like this?"

"They don't think they're doing anything wrong." She crushed her hands together in her lap. "Far from it. In fact, they fervently believe it's right."

"It's fucking scary."

"Huh," she said. "Never known you to get like this before."

"Like what?"

She nodded at the TV. "Current affairs, the news... all that doesn't usually bother you." Her brow furrowed. "What's it got to do with you? Us?"

Cameron straightened in his seat. "It's got everything to do with us. I mean..." He frowned. "Are you upset with me?"

"No." She vigorously rubbed her eyes. "Not upset. Just... disappointed, I guess. Didn't Beth say you were a closed book? You've changed, Cam."

He felt the skin crawl over the bone of his scalp. "Doesn't any of this worry you? I mean, the war in Syria..."

"We've all got our wars to fight." She bared small, stained teeth at him. "In here." She tapped her head with her forefinger. "Out there." She nodded in the direction of the window. "Everything needs fixing. None of it's right. Just ripples for the cataclysm to come."

He tried to take in the implication of her words. "I'm not saying we're perfect. I know our own lives and systems are flawed…"

"It needs tearing down and starting again," she snapped, her face twisting into a grotesque mask of hate. "Everything's decayed. Everything's wrong."

He sensed the walls shimmer strangely around him. She got up and left the room, slamming the door on her way out.

July, 2014

Cameron and Megan heaved their luggage into the hotel, straightened and let the rain slip down their tired, shivering faces. Cameron knuckled his eyes, eager to grab some much-needed sleep.

The lobby was half-lit by two green lamps, one on a wooden table by the door, the other on the reception desk next to a vase of freshly cut flowers. To their left, a staircase curled away into darkness.

"Blast." Megan dragged a hand through her hair. "I've left our overnight bag in the car."

"I'll get it." Cameron zipped up his coat. "You sort out the room."

He slipped back out of the hotel, rain crackling against his mac. He sprinted to Meg's Clio, swung open the front passenger door. Waited for a lightning flash to help locate the bag in the footwell. Moments later he was back inside, pulling the hotel doors closed behind him.

The lobby was deserted, Megan gone.

Behind the seething rain, Cameron could hear the faint hum of the lamps and the lonesome tick of the long-case clock in the corner.

"*Bon soir.*"

He wheeled, seeing a tall, willowy woman standing behind the wood panelled reception desk.

"*Votre ami est à l'étage*," she said.

He blinked twice, rapidly.

She sighed, then nodded toward the staircase.

"Up here?" he said, pointing.

"*Oui. A l'étage.*"

He climbed the stairs, then drifted along the carpeted first floor landing. Doors reared up around him, shadows pirouetted across walls. Two more green lamps shone, one on a bookcase, the other on a table and right at the end of the landing a window glowed every so often with reflected lightning.

He came upon a door that was ajar. He pressed against it, pushed hard. To his relief, Megan was inside, standing dead-still in front of a window.

He thought of the time in the Residents' Centre when her eyes had shone in that dark, back room.

"Meg?"

She threw a glance at him and he was relieved to see her eyes weren't shining now.

"Thanks," he huffed, kicking shut the door. "I really appreciate it when you run off like that."

Her gaze flickered back to the window. "Shush. Come and look. The storm's fantastic."

Blinding lights. Destructive forces. These things sang in her bones and burned through her veins.

He dumped the bag on the dressing table, then sat down on the bed behind her. The room was whitewashed, sparsely decorated. A wooden chair lurked in a corner, shrouded in darkness.

She reached out, lightly touching his knee. "What's the matter?"

"Why did you leave me like that?" He pulled off his coat. "The woman downstairs *talked* to me, Meg."

She tossed her head back and laughed, loudly.

"It's goddamn hot," he muttered, clawing at his shirt collar. "I thought the storm might clear the air." He winced at the irritation underscoring his words. The fear of the unknown, the anxiety of being in an unfamiliar place where he didn't speak the same language was all beginning to grate. "I find it difficult to communicate at the best of times," he said, not meaning to say it out loud.

Megan flashed him a strange, sad smile. "It's what you carry around inside that counts. We'll all get to express ourselves soon. *Then* people shall know."

Her eyes slowly filled with that mysterious light as a clap of thunder rattled the fragile silence of the room.

December, 2013

Nerves fluttered in Cameron's stomach. He was standing outside of the Residents' Centre, mulling

160

over how he'd come to be here. He remembered the card, viewed three days ago; stuck to the centre's window by pieces of Blu-Tack.

If you feel angry, lost, or scared, you're not alone. Come to our meetings - 7pm every Wednesday at the Residents' Centre, Crow Lane, Wickham.

His mind projected images of his flat – empty, silent, and dark – and that had decided it; he didn't want to be alone again tonight.

Drawing breath, he opened the door and stepped tentatively inside.

The room was bright and inviting. Furniture and play equipment had been pushed to one side. Sat in a circle in the middle of the room were six people who all looked up and around as he entered.

"H-hi," he stammered, raising his hand.

A bearded man with sharp grey eyes quickly rose, giving Cameron a polite bow. "Come in," he said, turning, lifting another chair from off a stack in the corner. "You're here for the group, right?"

"Yes." Cameron nodded, feeling the colour rise to his cheeks.

"Good. Oh, good." Relief passed across the man's face. "Please sit."

Cameron sat.

The man sank into the chair opposite him, then leapt up again, offering Cameron his hand. "I'm Patrick."

"Cameron."

"Nice to meet you, Cameron."

They shook hands, and Patrick sat back down. The guy seemed filled with nervous, infectious energy.

"Stephanie." Patrick turned to a young woman to his left. "Please, continue. You were saying?"

The woman tucked a strand of blonde hair behind her ear, throwing a cautious glance at Cameron. She shut her eyes briefly on them all before saying, "It's a power point in Rennes-le-Château. We know there are others – power distilled from the Ark and then contained within walls. And there are more containers now; walking carriers – the power contained in flesh."

The other members nodded, sagely.

"Things need to change," Stephanie continued, anger building in her voice. "We *have* to believe."

Another young woman who looked like Stephanie added, "Why do we want this? Because we hate and we want out. Nothing's fair, right? All we see is heartbreak, cruelty and injustice."

Patrick folded his arms across his chest, flashing a small, affectionate smile. "There is a better world," he said. "We know it. *Feel* it." His gaze drifted around the circle before finally focusing on Cameron. "Cameron, please introduce yourself. Tell us why you're here."

Cameron's cheeks burned. He sensed the group's eyes on him and stared at the palms of his hands for a moment. "I… I can't really pinpoint when and why things went wrong with Beth and I." He swallowed down a lump in his throat. "We were going through the motions, I guess. Safe in our habitual patterns and routines. Life was comfortable. Predictable, even.

"I first found out she was cheating when she accidentally left her laptop open. I think I knew, deep down, something wasn't right. That would explain why I trawled through her emails that day.

"I saw the messages – and that was the start of the end, really. She'd been living another life, searching for something that was missing from ours." He lowered his head, unable and unwilling to meet anyone's eyes.

"The divorce was messy. Poor Jess, our daughter. She was about to start her GCSEs, and of course her schooling suffered as a result. She hated Beth for what she'd done, for breaking up our family unit. I hated her, too. But that hate was tempered by guilt. Had I let her down as a husband?"

Beth momentarily appeared in his mind – red hair; freckles; that bright, pretty smile.

"I've always struggled to express my emotions. Beth said I was a closed book. When I found out she was cheating on me, my lack of reaction just concerned me into thinking I was more emotionally stunted than I thought."

He knitted his brows together as he carefully considered his next words.

"The court decided Beth would have Jess on weekends and I would have her during the week. Which was fine by me and Jess.

"Except... Jess's disdain for her mother never went away. And it came to the point where she didn't want to visit her mother at all."

163

Cameron closed his eyes, visualising his daughter's tear-streaked face in the darkness behind his lids.

"She was upset that Friday – the last time I saw her alive, I mean. She pleaded with me to let her stay home. Beth was living with another man, not even the same one she cheated on me with, in a house in the city centre.

"We sat in the car outside that house and Jess cried and cried. It was almost as though she *knew* something bad was going to happen. She usually got upset prior to me dropping her off, but never like this."

Cameron's voice sounded hoarse and hollow to his own ears.

"I reached out and shook her shoulder and told her everything was going to be fine, that she had to spend time with Beth because Beth had made plans for her... but secretly and selfishly I wanted her to go because I was craving a weekend alone, away from the responsibilities and pressures of being a parent."

The world seemed to be drifting from him, his body levitating from the moment. He blinked twice, rapidly, to dispel the notion. "I did love Jess. Loved her with all my heart. And when I think about the way she died..."

Screams. Smoke.

Panic.

Terror.

"She pleaded with me to take her back to my flat, but I told her to go. And I watched her walk sobbing, to that front door... and that was when I drove away." He clenched his hands, fingernails digging into the soft flesh of his palms.

"Then there was the fire. Beth's partner had fallen asleep with a cigarette in his hand and the whole house had gone up. Jess had been asleep in the spare bedroom at the time, and..."

He grabbed his face, breathing hard through his fingers. "I let her go into that house when she didn't want to. Now I have to live with that for the rest of my days."

Patrick leaned forward in his chair. "We're here to help. To listen. Remember – you're not alone."

The woman to Cameron's right, Megan, briefly touched his arm. "You *know*. You understand. You're one of us now." He could smell her perfume – something sweet and exotic – and found it oddly reassuring. He had no idea why.

When it was time to finish, Cameron helped the others pull the tables forward and stack the chairs.

"You will come back, won't you?" asked a middle-aged woman with thick red lipstick smeared around her mouth.

"You're not alone," reiterated a tall, nervous-looking man with glasses.

Cameron stepped out into the cold, then collapsed against a wall, sighing, shaking his head. He couldn't believe he'd opened up like that, in front of complete strangers, too. He heard a cough, and quickly turned. Patrick was outside, smoking a cigarette by a shattered telephone box. Inside the centre, Megan, Stephanie, and another blonde were nattering away to each other in a corner. They

165

appeared animated, kept glancing through the window at Cameron.

Patrick saw Cameron looking.

"My daughters." He raised his hand and waved at them. They waved back.

"All three?" Cameron asked.

"Yep." Patrick grimaced around his cigarette. "Can't imagine what you've been through. I'm really sorry, Cameron."

Cameron struggled to formulate a reply.

Patrick took one last puff on his cigarette, then flicked it away into the darkness. "When I was your age, I had no purpose. I drank too much, didn't look after myself at all. Like you, I was in a non-reciprocal relationship. We had the girls, but nothing in common." He rubbed his nose with the back of his hand. "Then, one day, I took them away." An odd laugh escaped him. "I got into trouble for that." He glanced at the Residents' Centre again. "But I knew best and in the end my girls came to me like moths to a light."

"You must be proud."

"I am." Patrick zipped his coat up to his neck. "There's still something left of Clara, though. Some small *sliver*. She clings to it, despite our... efforts."

Cameron was just about to ask what she was clinging to when the door opened behind him. He turned to see the three women emerge from the centre. They looked similar. Piercing grey eyes. Long blonde hair. The same high cheekbones and thin, crooked mouth.

"Good to meet you." Patrick stuck out his hand. Cameron shook it. "Will you be back? We'd very much like it, Cameron."

Cameron forced a smile. "Sure."

He was dimly aware of the girls whispering to each other as he left. He rounded a corner by the chip shop, hurried down Blackhart Hill. Streetlamps painted terraces, cars slithered past him. A group of youths in hoodies shared a bottle of cider inside a tag-sprayed bus shelter.

He crossed the street, then turned when he heard his name being called.

One of the women was racing down the hill, waving her arms.

Megan.

"Sorry," she said, reaching him, panting. She quickly got her breath back. "Didn't mean to startle you."

"You didn't. You okay?"

She tugged at the collar of her blouse. "I feel... *silly*."

"Why?"

"It's just..." Her arms fell limply to her sides. "I hope you don't think me forward. I've always been spontaneous, and..." She rolled her eyes. "God, I'm rambling here, aren't I?" She laughed, shrilly. Then, clearing her throat, composing herself, she said: "You're not like the others. I mean, the people who usually come through our door. I knew it as soon as I set eyes on you."

Her lips formed a coy smile. "I find you attractive. There. Said it."

He stared at her.

That smile. The piercing eyes. The smell of her perfume.

It awakened something inside him that he thought was long dead.

April, 2014

They emerged from the cinema, their eyes struggling to adapt to the daylight. The street was busy, bustling and squirming with shoppers.

"Well, that was… odd." Cameron buttoned his coat up.

Megan's heels clacked on the concrete beside him. "Very," she agreed.

Cameron's head was filled with black rooms, dark pools and weird forests. He'd appreciated the passive air Scarlett Johansson had exuded, but the film itself had been unsettling and strange.

"I didn't like it." Megan hitched her handbag up over her shoulder. "It was such a cold experience."

"Think that was the whole point of it."

"But that's how I feel about *all* films." He looked at her, and her sad smile told him she was being serious. "Same for music and books. I don't get them, Cam."

"You don't get them?" He laughed warily, shaking his head from side-to-side. "It's going to be tough thinking up date ideas with you."

She shrugged. "I'm just happy to be with you, that's all."

They resumed walking, a taut silence stretching between them. Suddenly feeling the need to talk,

Cameron said, "You honestly don't like films? Going to the cinema was a weekly highlight for me when I was a kid."

"There's nothing these things can ever teach me, because there's only The Way."

There it is again, he thought, turning his face away before she could say anything more.

She gripped his arm, drawing him back to her. "Sorry, I'm sorry." She clawed a hand through her hair. "I'm not much fun, am I? It's just... I want to be with you. And I'm desperate to show you what *I've* experienced. What I've seen. There's no room in my head for anything else. But if I can share it..."

"Show me, then."

Her face brightened. She nodded and they linked arms and pushed on, through the crowd. "Emotions are dumb things. They enslave us. Make us weak."

"What about the flip side? Don't you ever feel good about yourself?"

She chewed her lip. "Only when I'm around you," she replied.

They arrived at the flat just as it was getting dark. Cameron let them in with his key. He closed the door behind them, thoughts festering in his mind.

Was it the right time to broach Shining Way? To finally get his feelings off of his chest? There was so much he wasn't sure about, not least the way *they* were controlling Megan.

A cork popped. Megan stepped out of the kitchen with two glasses of bubbly. They sat on the

169

settee and stretched their legs out. Headlamps from the traffic outside swept through the room.

Megan touched his face.

Say something, he thought. But she spoke before he could. "Got something for you."

"Oh?"

She nodded at the coffee table.

There was a brown envelope on it, partially hidden by a TV-listings magazine. "Open it."

He scooped up and tore open the envelope, extracting the printouts inside. He scanned them, realising it was confirmation bookings for a ferry to Bilbao and a hotel room in Rennes-le-Château for six nights.

She flung her arms around his neck, laughing, nibbling his ear. He couldn't ruin this moment by expressing doubt; he knew she'd get upset with him. He'd have to go along with it, see what she wanted him to see. Which meant having to abandon their little chat about Shining Way for now.

She took the paperwork from him and put it back on the coffee table. "Dad bought it for us."

Of course, Cameron thought. *Patrick. Who else?*

"Stay there." She jumped up and headed for the kitchen, returning moments later with the champagne bottle. She topped them both up. "To France," she said, their glasses chinking together.

"To France."

She put the bottle down on the floor. Snuggled into him and played with his hair. She'd want to go to bed soon.

170

She drew back suddenly, her eyes tight and worried. "You're very quiet."

"Been thinking about my dreams again."

"What've you been dreaming this time?"

"Don't know." He shrugged. "Don't tend to remember much about them, to be honest. Just the feelings they leave behind, I guess." His mouth managed to shape itself into a smile. "I tend to wake up... *exhausted* from them."

She touched his face softly, deftly, then dropped her hand onto the settee. "You know I can manipulate dreams, don't you?" She let out a small, playful giggle. "With my magic rays, I can erase thoughts and memories. You're under my spell, Cam. Under my complete control and command."

He stared at her for a long moment. Then, quietly chuckling to himself, he pulled her in close, drawing in the scent of her perfume, her hair. "You're a strange one," he said. "Scarlett Johansson's got nothing on you."

Part II

"When the time comes, we'll shine like stars.
"The world doesn't owe us a thing, remember?
"Sear it away. Sear it all away.
"Let's burn it down and start again."

July, 2014

Megan and Cameron picnicked in a small, pretty village a mile or so north of Rennes-le-Château. There was some sort of festival going on, the streets decked out with banners, streamers and flags. They sat in the heart of the village, on a bench in the shade, eating crepes and ice-cream from white plastic bowls.

Enthusiastic French voices barked from Tannoy speakers lashed to streetlamps, the language barrier reminding Cameron of the funeral and how, during his eulogy, he had struggled to convey his loss.

He put his bowl down, watching Megan's hand creep across the bench toward him. Taking his hand, she weaved her fingers between his and squeezed.

"I was thinking about Jess," he said, hunching up so that she couldn't see his face. "What I'd do to see her again, Meg."

Megan was quiet, like he knew she would be.

People moved about them, carrying hotdogs and plastic cups filled with beer. Birds chattered from telegraph wires, litter skipped and danced about their feet. Finally, Cameron met her gaze.

Her eyes were cold, hard, and unblinking.

"What was one of the first things I taught you?" She wormed her hand free of his, dropping it behind her back. "The world's not fair, life's not fair. It's what we're fighting against, right?" She puffed out her cheeks. "All we have is the belief there's a better world."

He nodded absently, his thoughts wandering.

Megan, Shining Way, The Light – what did it all mean? These days, he was too scared to contemplate, too afraid to think where they might take him. "We've got each other," he said.

His cheeks coloured when she laughed and he looked down to hide his embarrassment.

She lowered her head so he could see her, a pitying smile creeping across her face. "You're a sweetheart, you know that? One of the good ones." The smile vanished and she glared almost conspiratorially around them. "You talk about you and me and it's beautiful, Cam, it really is. But things'll be *different* soon. Us, together... that's *selfish* talk." She gripped his arm, fingernails digging into his flesh. "There's a change coming. I know you don't understand." That smile snaked across her face again. "You will."

She got up and walked away before he could reply. He found his feet, following her toward a cluster of rickety, decrepit-looking buildings. His mind was racing, his thoughts muddled by the intense heat and humidity. Megan was changing, taking control of his world once more.

They found a small, ivy-clad church at the bottom of a lane. There was no door, just a black square in the wall, like an entrance to a cave. Megan stooped, disappearing into darkness. Cameron, palming sweat from off his face, followed her inside.

Cool air enveloped him, a welcome respite from the stifling heat. His gaze focused, picking out wooden effigies of saint-like figures in the darkness, their hands pressed together, their eyes painted a gaudy silver. Candle flames wavered in small, shallow alcoves. A stained-glass window set in the farthest wall depicted an image of a man with rays of light shooting from his mouth and eyes.

There were three murals dressing the wall opposite. Cameron squinted and stared, quickly ascertaining what each one represented.

The first depicted the Israelites carrying the Ark of the Covenant through a desert, toward the banks of the River Jordan, the Ark hidden beneath a veil made of skins and blue cloth.

The second showed King David bringing the Ark to Jerusalem.

The third depicted the Virgin Mary with her arms stretched out in benediction, her wide eyes shining like stars.

A hand gripped his arm.

He turned to see an elderly man in robes and a clerical collar, his countenance a road-map of lines, scars, and wrinkles.

"Soldat." The old priest grinned, specks of light dancing in his rheumy eyes. "*Soldat.*"

Cameron broke away, hurrying to Megan's side. She was staring at dozens of photographs pinned above an altar in the corner. Dust whirled in the half-lit space between them, forming and re-forming new worlds. "Meg?"

She blinked and smiled at him. "Look," she said, pointing excitedly. Cameron looked at the photos, noting they all depicted the same crumbling chapel by the side of a long and deserted country road. "*Lieu de lumière.*" A dreamy smile passed across her face.

He grabbed hold of her arm. "Can we go, please?"

They stepped back out into the raging sunshine. Cameron's senses felt flooded, laughter from a group of tourists serving only to heighten his disorientation.

"The priest." He paced the spot, rubbing his brow with his fingers. "That priest in the church… He said something to me just now."

Megan gave a cryptic little smile. "He called you 'soldier'." He stared blankly at her. "Let's go in here."

She led him by the hand through a rust-eaten gate into a small, neglected churchyard. They sat on a bench in the shade, staring at ancient headstones and crosses slicing out of the overgrowth.

"Why are we here?" Cameron wiped his sleeve across his forehead.

"You'll see." She twirled a long length of her hair with her fingers until one by one the strands slipped from her grasp. "It's the final jump of the hoop. An initiation. A pilgrimage, if you like."

175

He grimaced, sweat trickling down the length of his face.

"Hey," she said, nudging him. "Let's go out for dinner tonight." Her pale lips twitched into a grin. "Then I can reveal to you why we're here. The *real* reason, Cam."

March, 2014

Just before 7PM, Cameron arrived at the Residents' Centre for another group meet-up. The same faces were there – Patrick and his three daughters, Stephanie, Clara, and Megan. The two other regular attendees were absent, no new faces had come through the door for weeks.

Cameron took off his jacket, folding it over the back of a chair. Megan was seated beside him, rocking from side-to-side, a spaced-out smile all over her face. He shook her arm gently, tenderly, but she didn't react at all.

He'd seen her like this before. The first time he thought she was on something. Patrick had to take him to one side and explain it was a form of meditation – of 'tuning in' to the light.

Under her breath she was whispering something, the words uttered in a quiet, sing-song voice. *"Light through the veins, light through the veins…"*

Patrick and Stephanie were smiling, but Clara was locked inside herself, tugging at her hair, staring down at the floor.

Patrick sermonised for a while, revealing: "The things we see! The stuff we *dream*. It's mind-blowing, Cameron, it really is!" Under the fluorescent glare of the strip-lights, his smile looked vaguely grotesque. "You're here because you want it, too."

No, Cameron thought. *I'm here for Megan. She brought me back from the dead. Got me to think and feel again. I'm not interested in your bullshit, whatever it is you believe in. The only thing I believe in is Meg.*

Suddenly, Clara spoke; spinning in her seat, she shrieked at Cameron – "Don't think she cares! All this *empathy* and understanding is -"

"Enough!" Patrick was quickly on his feet, bending at the waist, whispering to Clara: "What's got into you? You need to stop this – *now.*"

Silence.

Megan flopped back into her seat, a wry smile stitched to her lips. Stephanie averted her gaze to the wall.

Should Cameron say something? Ask what this was about? He opened his mouth, but thought better of it. This had nothing to do with him. He felt temporarily locked out. Lost.

Clara got to her feet, then made her way to the storeroom, slamming the door shut behind her. Megan rocked forwards, turning her face away and sniggering. Patrick and Stephanie took their coffee mugs over to the sink to wash up. Their collective silence felt awkward and tense.

Cameron turned to Megan. "You coming to mine tonight?"

"No," she whispered. "Not tonight. I'm staying with my sisters this evening."

He shot up from his seat, approaching Patrick and Stephanie at the sink. Megan resumed chanting and singing behind him.

Patrick frowned. "You okay, Cameron?"

"Just thinking about leaving. It's a long walk home for me."

"Sorry about Clara." Patrick put a hand on his shoulder. "She gets like that sometimes. Jealousy, I think. She's always wanted what her sisters have got. It's not her fault, not really. She *was* the last to go in."

Cameron raised his eyebrows in puzzlement. "The last to go in?"

"By then I expect the power had diminished somewhat. We'll take her back one day."

"You've lost me."

Patrick nodded at Megan. "We'll look after her tonight, Cameron."

Cameron turned to face Megan again.

Her eyelids were fluttering in perfect synchronicity with the flickering of the strip-light above her head.

He left them then. Walked out of the building and into the night. A waft of fried food and grease from the chip shop filled his nostrils. Car headlamps washed across the pavement. Kids laughing in a bus shelter helped anchor him to the world, establishing a sense of normality again.

Both Megan and Clara's behaviour had greatly disturbed him tonight. *Don't think she cares!* Christ, what had Clara *meant* by that? Perhaps Patrick was right and it had all been a simple display of jealously on her part.

Cameron stopped abruptly, rubbing his arms and shivering. He'd left his jacket behind. If he was quick enough, he could run up and get it.

He climbed Blackhart Hill again, passing the convenience store and bus shelter. Perhaps Megan would change her mind and come on home with him, he thought, hopefully.

He arrived back at the centre. Clara was sitting and sobbing on her chair. Patrick was crouched beside her, whispering: "… only The Light remains." Stephanie was standing over them and all three looked up and around as he entered.

He felt like he was intruding and immediately blushed. "Sorry. Forgot my jacket."

"It's all right, Cameron." Patrick straightened up, smiling.

Cameron hurried to his chair, scooped up his jacket. Patrick was staring at him with no discernible expression on his face at all. "Where's Megan?"

"She's in the storeroom." Patrick clasped his hands together in front of him, rocking backwards and forwards on his heels. "She's very tired."

Cameron approached the back door. "I didn't say goodbye. I'll just…"

"No. She's fine. Leave her."

Was there a hint of panic to his voice?

"Two minutes."

Patrick stepped forward to intercept, but Cameron was already opening and moving through the back door. He slipped into a small, square corridor. To his right, the entrance to the toilet; to his left, the storeroom's grey, unpainted door.

He twisted its handle, pushing at the same time.

The lights were off inside. Toys and play apparatus were lurking mounds of shadow. Over in the corner, Megan was standing in front of the window, her hands spread out against the glass.

"Meg?"

He froze, then put his hand over his mouth.

Her eyes were glowing, *shining*, painting that small section of the room with light. As she whispered to herself, scores of moths fluttered and flickered beyond the pane.

He closed the door on her, breathing deep, trying to compose himself. Then, swiftly shaking his head, he wheeled and returned to the centre's main room.

Patrick and Stephanie looked around at him. They were over by the sink again. Cameron crossed the room, pushing through the front door. He saw Clara outside, lingering beside the vandalised telephone box.

"I saw Meg," he told her, his voice shaky, faint. "Her eyes... The moths..."

Clara stepped forward, her pale face emerging from the darkness.

"Ever wondered why moths stay at lights?" she asked. Cameron could only shake his head in reply. "A moth's eyes have sensors. They adjust according to the amount of light they detect." Her face glittered brightly with tears. "A moth's dark-adapting mechanism responds slower than its light-adapting mechanism. So, once the moth comes to a light, it finds it difficult to return... to the dark, I mean. They're blind for ages. They can't pull themselves away." She cupped a hand over her mouth, then took it away again. "Neither will you."

July, 2014

The sun was sinking, the sky a dark, smouldering violet. Stars glinted behind rows of inanimate cypress trees. They sat in the outside area of a restaurant, under a green plastic canopy. Megan ordered mussels, Cameron an omelette. As they waited for their meals, Megan checked the GPS on her phone. "Not far now." She put the phone back down on the table and smiled at him.

The smile vanished. "What's wrong, Cam?"

Cameron was on the verge of full-blown panic. Something was screaming for him to leave; to abandon Megan and this weird pilgrimage immediately.

He abruptly stood.

"Where are you going?"

"The rest room." He pushed his chair in. "Won't be long."

He stumbled to the back of the restaurant, along a crumbling path strewn with weeds. The trees bowed over a low wall, thin and skeletal in the gloaming. He reached the outhouse, pushed through the door. Staggered to a slime-encrusted basin and vomited, violently, into it. Seconds later, he lifted his head. A cracked mirror above the sink distorted his features, pulling his eyes askew.

He twisted a tap, cupped his hands under it. Splashed cold water onto his face. Soon, the nausea passed. He straightened, wiping vomit away from his mouth. "You're okay," he whispered. "It'll all be okay."

He could slip away without her noticing. Just climb the wall, walk out across the fields and leave; it was as simple as that. Instead, he placed a hand on the basin and squeezed shut his eyes.

Where are you?

He was finding it increasingly hard to visualise his daughter's face now. Why couldn't he picture it anymore? Why wasn't it there?

"You okay?" Megan asked as soon as he returned to their table.

He sat back down in his seat. "Sure."

The waiter arrived before she could say anything more, putting their plates of food down in front of them. Megan pushed her mobile into her pocket, tucked a loose strand of hair behind her ear.

Later, as they ate, he asked, "So, what is it we're looking for?"

Part III

"Don't look at me.

"I don't want you to see me like this. You're not ready. You wouldn't understand.

"Sleep. Go back to your dreams. They'll prepare you for the searing."

June, 2014

"DAD!"

Jess.

Oh, shit.

Jess.

He gripped the handrail, bounding up the stairs, smoke surrounding him in a thick cocoon of floating embers and scorching ash. He had to keep going – couldn't stop now.

Three-quarters of the way up, he spotted Jess through the smoke. He braced himself, then plunged through the flames, coughing, spluttering, reaching. Heat blasted. Fire seared. He gripped Jess's shoulder, turned her to him. "Got you," he gasped. "Got you, thank God."

It wasn't Jess.

Megan was standing there instead, grinning at him.

He stumbled backwards, surprised, disorientated. As the smoke withdrew, he realised they weren't in a house at all, but his flat, his sitting room. He dropped his hands to his sides and stared at her, then looked helplessly around.

He was just about to ask where Jess was when Megan said, quietly, "Come and look," and led him by the hand over to the window.

The sky was on fire.

It looked like it was about to fall and burn the city to a cinder at any given moment.

She tossed her head back and laughed, loudly.

"Wonderful," she said. "Isn't it?"

May, 2014

"…and it works kind of like a battery. It needs time to charge. It's an amazing…"

Megan was leaning over him, whispering softly, her fingers lightly brushing his face.

His eyelids cracked open.

"Morning," she smiled.

He sat up, the bed creaking beneath him. "What were you saying just then?" He kneaded his eyes with his fists and yawned. "You were saying something just now. Something about…"

"You were dreaming."

"Christ," he said, shaking his head, "think I'm more tired now than I was when I went to bed."

"Seven more weeks," she giggled.

A scowl twisted his features. He pushed Megan aside and clambered out of bed.

"What shall we do today?" she asked him.

"I should start looking for a job." He grabbed some fresh jeans and a T-shirt. "Start contributing to society again."

He knew she wouldn't like that.

Perhaps it was her rant yesterday about the news on TV that had darkened his mood, but he really didn't like her much at the moment.

"Why?" She flicked her hair out of her eyes. "We've enough money to get by on. We don't need much."

"I'm stagnating."

"All the better to get away, then." She breathed out an exasperated sigh. "Everything will seem so much clearer after our break."

He pulled on his clothes, throwing a guilty glance back at her. "I don't want to go."

There, he thought. *Said it.* She winced and sat up, a swift shadow of anger sweeping across her face. "Then you'll be denying yourself!" she hissed. "If you want to be a sad little nobody, then that's your business. You'll come and go like the rest of them." Her cheekbones twitched, her eyes blazed. "Don't you want to be part of something *better*? Part of something different, amazing, and... *eternal*?"

He took a deep breath before saying, "That's the problem. You keep me in the dark all the time. You never let me in on what's going on." His voice cracked. He swiftly rubbed his eyes to stem the tears.

She kicked off the duvet, leaped up, and rushed over to him, flinging her arms around his neck. "When are you going to realise you're looking at this the wrong way?" she cried. "You've got yourself all worked up, haven't you? You need to view it from a different angle – see the bigger picture! I can't help you anymore, not until we're *there*." She drew back, looking him straight in the eye. "You're doing this for me, remember? Because you're a lovely man. Because you like me. And I like you. You don't have to be alone anymore." She hardened her voice. "Never lose sight of your hate. Shape your pain and despair into a weapon of *truth*. We've a message to send, and the world needs to hear it, Cam."

July, 2014

"Shouldn't we be going back to the hotel?" Cameron asked, glancing around at Megan as she drove. They passed dark fields, dilapidated barns and black, shapeless farmhouses. "It's getting late."

"Not yet," she whispered, eyes fixed on the road ahead.

Just outside of Rennes-le-Château, she flicked the indicator stem and pulled up into a layby. She cranked the handbrake, nodding out of the window at a chapel on the other side of the road. "Go in there," she said. "*Please,* Cam."

He couldn't drag his gaze away from her face. "The chapel?" He emitted a quiet, uneasy laugh. "That's the one in the photographs. The ones in the church we visited, right?"

"Please. No questions. Just go inside."

He gave an assenting nod, then sighed and opened the front passenger door.

The moon glowed over the chapel's steeply pitched roof. Crickets sang. Stars glinted between the knotted branches of a dead yew.

He crossed the road, opened an iron gate and edged down a path to the chapel's arched wooden door. Pinned or placed on a ledge above the entrance were photographs, colourful-looking beads, silver lockets and strands of hair in small, polythene bags.

Carved into the wood of the door were the words *Lieu de lumière*.

"Power distilled from the Ark and then contained within walls."

His thoughts churned as he paused before the entryway.

Taking all he'd heard and learnt into consideration, this place had the potential to change him. He was already broken; what else did he have to lose?

He closed his eyes, searching for Jess in the darkness behind his lids. But again, the blackness was too heavy, the features of her face too ill-defined.

With my magic rays, I can erase thoughts and memories.

He reopened his eyes. Grit his teeth and pushed through the door.

The moon spread its light onto an altar covered by a blue sheet with white stars and hook-shaped moons patterned across it. There was a small table and a chair in front of the altar. A cracked statue of a saint lurked in one corner, its pale hands clasped together, its eyes painted a gaudy silver.

The air crackled with unnatural energy, causing the hairs on the back of his neck to stand on end.

Pilgrimage.

Initiation.

Baptism.

Those words exploded like fireworks inside his skull.

He didn't have to be here. It wasn't too late to turn back. But without Jess and Beth, what did he have?

"Megan," he whispered.

Megan.

Perhaps he really was under her control. Maybe he was being used. But she was all he had now; there was nobody else.

He closed the door, then groped for the chair and sat. His breath came in thick, strangled rasps. His heart thudded and thundered. Something, he sensed, was in the room with him, slowly beginning to form, to manifest – wanting to replace so much of him with itself.

The darkness cracked right open, arrows of bright, blinding, pure, white light suddenly shooting out and striking him a dozen times in quick succession.

He was knocked to his feet, a shrill noise ringing in his ears; it took a moment or two for him to realise it was the sound of his own screaming.

He found and flung open the door. Megan was standing outside, waiting by the iron gate, her eyes wide and startled-looking. She moved quickly to him, gripping his arm, helping him across the road to her Clio. She opened the passenger door, then sat him down and secured the seatbelt. He was sweating profusely, burning up and shivering.

She leapt into the driver's seat. Drove quickly away, the markings in the road soon flashing and skipping beneath them again.

She glanced at him. Bit down hard on her lip before refocusing on the road.

"We came along this way," she said, "after Mum left Dad. Dad – Patrick – took us here without Mum knowing. He wanted to take us away from all that was false... all that was *weak*." She gripped the wheel until her knuckles whitened. "We stopped there, at that place. Dad went in first. Then we all did – me; my sisters, Steph and Clara."

She pulled in a sharp breath. "That place... it spoke to us. To *all* of us... to varying degrees." Cameron thought of Clara. *There's still something left. Some small* sliver.

Megan fell silent again. The markings continued to skip and flash under them. Cameron couldn't speak, couldn't even bring himself to look at her. He lifted his head and saw his eyes were shining from his reflection in the windscreen.

"You've been there." Megan's frail voice trembled. "You've experienced it. It's *good*... right?"

Cameron slunk down in his seat and, covering his face with his hands, wept and sobbed until only The Light remained.

High Stakes
A Vampire Detective Mystery

Terrance V. Mc Arthur

Chapter One
A Wake-Up Call

Cell phones are nasty things. They're always invading your life, letting people that you don't want to talk to find you in places you have gone to avoid them and it's really annoying when they ring in your coffin.

Yeah. That's right. The phone was ringing in my coffin.

I'm a vampire. I used to be a police detective, but that was before I was "kicked" –turned into a vampire—you know, like in "kicked the bucket" and "kicked over the old supper dish." Now, I'm a private investigator.

Anyway, I started out this story by expressing my feelings about cell phones, because one of those undesirable inventions was ringing in my coffin. It must have been only moments after sundown; it was the first thing I was aware of when my day-sleep ended. Even though my coffin is lined and padded, that clanging sound in a confined space is not pleasant to a still-fuzzy brain. I popped the phone, gathered all the intelligence I could find in my head, and said:

"Hunh?"

A shaky, male-ish voice asked, "Is this Mr. Carl—Sanger?"

"It's Sangre. *Sahn*-gray."

"Sorry, Mr. Sangre. I'm Austin Dunn. I work for Sandor. He gave me this number to call if anything happened."

"Fine," I said and waited for him to continue. When he didn't, I asked, "What happened?"

"It's Sandor. He's dead."

I thought about that for three seconds. "So what? I've known him for years and I've never known him when he wasn't dead."

Sandor was centuries old, one of the first blood-drinkers to reach the New World from the Carpathia-Transylvania region. There was a quiet time on the line and then, "I mean, he's—gone."

That got me to open the lid of the coffin.

"Are you sure?"

"I just... know."

OK, the kid was bloodlinked to Sandor and he felt the death. Austin was a "ren," connected to his vampire by ties of blood, like the servant Renfield in the old Dracula book. Some masters in the Community used it like slavery, but Sandor was known as more of a mentor.

I climbed out while I asked, "Austin? Okay.. Where are you?"

"In the studio. Outside his chamber."

"Have you gone inside?"

"No."

"Good. Stay out," I told him. "Wait for me outside the building, at the curb."

191

Sandor Cusak didn't live in some impressive mansion. His home was the top floor of an old factory, next to the tracks. It wasn't a desirable neighborhood, but image was important to Sandor. He insisted on playing the eccentric artist, even if the old veindrainer was secretly rich enough to buy and sell the Trump Tower with one accountant tied behind his back.

He would live his life as a painter or sculptor for a few decades, drink less blood to make himself look older and less healthy, then "die" for a couple of years, hiding out until he was ready to return to the art world as an emerging talent. In a reminiscing mood, he once told me, "La Giocanda, the painting English-speakers call the Mona Lisa. You know why I painted her with that half-smile, the one people say is 'enigmatic?' If she had really smiled, you would have seen her fangs."

Sandor was a major member of the Community, the vampires and other once-humans and semi-humans and never-were-humans who— for lack of a better word—live in the city. There are a lot of us—not enough to swing an election, but more than you would expect, working in all sorts of jobs: actors, janitors, chefs, musicians, bartenders, writers, night watchmen, disc jockeys, artists, all-night gas station attendants and even a few police officers.

Someone has to keep a city that never has time to sleeps running through the night and coffins don't come cheap. We're there in the darkness, anyway, so we might as well make ourselves useful. I still fight crime in the city, solving cases and bringing the guilty to justice for the Council that governs the Community. Of course, vampire justice isn't always the same as what the living would expect under the U.S. Constitution; it's often bloodier, and it can be cruel, but—sometimes—it's more just.

Austin was waiting on the smudged, paint-stained sidewalk, right where I'd told him to be. Red hair sticking out in all directions, a freckle convention on his nose and cheeks, skinny and tall, dressed in serious-artist black, with wire-rimmed glasses: pretty much what I'd expected.

I don't know if I was what Austin expected. I wouldn't call myself tall, dark and handsome. I'm more of not-quite-short-enough to be short, I wound up with more of the Caucasian side of my Latino-Anglo heritage and my mother thought I was cute.

"Mr. Sangre?"

"That's right, but call me Carl. Let's go in, Austin." We entered the building through the warehouse level, boarded the freight elevator and started up to the studio.

I leaned against a side slat asked, "When did it happen?"

"About an hour before sundown," Austin said. "I was making sure I had everything set out for work—Sandor likes to get started as soon as it's dark—and I was holding on to a chair when it hit—the pain—and then I felt—empty. Sandor wasn't in my mind, heart, soul, whatever. He was—gone. In

193

his desk, I found the card with your number. I called you—and then the Council."

He'd done what he was supposed to do, so everybody who was supposed to know, knew. Something odd about his narrative, but I didn't know what and when something doesn't fit with the rest of the story, it makes sense to find out why it doesn't make sense. "Why were you holding a chair before you felt anything?"

"Oh, that?" He pointed outside the building and said, "When the trains come through, there's a lot of vibration in the workspace. It helps to grab something for extra stability."

That bit of information was punctuated with the crunch and thud of the elevator slowing to a halt at the top of the shaft. My dark-vision would have been enough for me, but Austin was still mostly human. He threw a switch and ceiling-hung lights lit up the area. I flinched a little, but relaxed when I realized that they were all good-old, Edison-style, incandescent bulbs, which are hard to get these days. There were no CFL fluorescents; I don't like them—they make my skin crawl. Really. To me, it feels like something is moving across my flesh and that's the first sign of a sunburn. It's the ultraviolet rays that get to me.

I'm not too crazy about daylight, either, but I can endure the morning sun for up to an hour, if I have a really good sunscreen, maybe SPF 101. Of course, I wouldn't be at my best, like a frat-boy who pulled an all-nighter to cram for a test on the same night as his fellow Greeks threw a kegger.

194

Hanging in the air, propped against the walls or laid out on the floor, Sandor's oversized canvases got your attention. Museums and galleries clamored for them. Collectors went in hock to own them. I looked at them, but was drawn to a small set of paintings near the door to Sandor's chamber. I pointed at them. "Your work?"

"Yes."

"Nice."

The kid had talent. Sandor usually chose good artists for protégés. With his tutoring, some of them made it to great and some of them became vampires. At the chamber entry, Austin tapped in a security code on a keypad and I told him, "I'll need you to stay out here."

"Okay." He stepped aside as soon the entrance to Sandor's day-crypt opened.

I gloved up, closed the thick door behind me and enjoyed the near-total silence. I let my dark-vision take a look around the room. Thick, black curtains covered the walls. The floor was a black, lustrous marble. At my second step, gas-fed torches flared into flame; motion sensors, nice touch. Ahead of me, black steps rose to a platform holding The Coffin. I didn't go up the steps, because I was looking at the right-side wall and a five-foot square painting that did not belong here.

It was delicate. It was frou-frou. It was sweet. It was not Sandor's work, or anything I could imagine him owning. Why would Sandor have THAT as the first thing he would see when he woke up in the evening? I don't know much about art, but THAT was hideous. On top of it all, the thing wasn't straight. It hung at a slight angle.

I finally pulled my gaze from the artistic horror on the wall. The Coffin was Sandor's only work that wasn't for the museums or the collectors; it was a personal piece, made for him by himself. Centuries-old wood, adorned with the brushstrokes of a dozen eras, Renaissance, Impressionism, Rococo, Cubism, Ashcan Realism and Post-Modernism. All his styles were melded and displayed in one piece. It was beautiful, except for one thing.

The long, black stake piercing the lid.

Chapter Two
Staked: The Gathering

The wooden stake appeared to be made of ebony. The top was smooth and shiny, with a waxy feel. I wasn't eager to open the coffin lid, but I knew I had to do it. It took some effort, even for a reasonably-healthy vampire like me. When the lid came loose, there wasn't much to see.

Sandor had rotted down to the dust-and-bits-of-bone level, his satin nightwear coated in the powder and ash of his sudden decomposition. I saw no signs of a struggle. If Austin's timeframe was right, Sandor was still in day-sleep when it happened and who expects a wooden stake to come slamming through your coffin lid and into your body, anyway? The centuries caught up with him in moments. The tip of the ebony was splintered and cracked; it had pierced all the way into the coffin bottom, which explained why the lid was hard to open.

Before I replaced the top, I bagged some samples of the remains, enough for DNA testing. I was confident the bits and pieces I could see were the remnants of Sandor, but the Council always liked to make sure. After all, more than one vampire tried to fake his ultimate death as a way of getting out of unpaid debts.

Habits from my days on the police force compelled me to give the place a careful examination and do a perimeter search; you never know what rolls into a corner, or what hides behind a curtain. Sandor had quite a cleaning service, or his ren was very good with a broom, because there wasn't anything of note—until I caught a slight billowing of the curtains on the side opposite the out-of-plumb waste of pigment.

A vampire can move very quietly and I soon stood in position. I whipped the black drapery up and away to reveal... a window, slightly open.

I took a look, but nothing immediately caught my eye, which meant I needed a different point of view. I'm not able to turn into a bat, but I can climb walls without breaking a sweat (or a nail) and my jumping? I'm no Superman, but I am able to leap small sheds at a single bound. After opening the window some more, I scuttled out onto the brickwork, leaning out over the street, scanning in all directions. A fire escape zig-zagged down from the roof, maybe ten feet to my left. I pondered each look, mentally sifting the view for things that were out of place. There was a gleam at the edge of my sight. I pivoted and scampered over the sill, back into Sandor's private sector of the loft and the safety of the dark curtain folds.

Across the street and a bit higher, a movement, a moment of light and a window returned to dark stillness. I waited—vampires can be very patient—but nothing over there waved at me. I relaxed and considered possibilities.

Could someone have inched his way along the ledge from the ladder and pried open the window? I noticed no signs of forced entry, just an open window. In daysleep, Sandor would not detect an intruder... or would his motion sensors have triggered an alert? A question to ask Austin.

I approached the door, becoming aware of vague sounds, muffled thumps and raised voices. I opened the door to find a petite, blue-streaked blonde grabbing Austin's shirt, lifting him into the air and slamming him against the wall, shouting, "What did you do? What did you do to him? What... [slam]... did... [slam]...you.. [slam]...?"

"Stop it, Rhetta," I said. "Put him down."

"Carl," she said as she let Austin slide to the floor. "I felt it. It ripped me out of my sleep, and my body had no power to do anything. I felt the pain, the shock. I dropped back into day-sleep, knowing—I felt him die!"

"I felt him die, too!" Austin stumbled to his feet, favoring his left side.

Rhetta Golding wasn't finished with him. I might not be allowing her to hit him, but she kept jabbing at Austin, verbally.

She demanded, "Tell me! What were you doing that was so important that you could let someone waltz in here, kill him, and leave?"

"I was right here," he told her, "and nobody else was here, all day long."

"Did you do it?" She accused him with, "You were jealous of him and you wanted—"

"Sandor gave me all I wanted and more. He was my hero, my master, my friend, my second father, my teacher, my—I loved him, more than you ever did!" He pointed a finger, accusing right back at her, "You used him! You used your time as a ren to get connections, to get fame, to get power. Well, you've got it. You were kicked, turned, got your fangs. You're the new Great Vampire Art Hope. How do you like it?"

I hated to interrupt this loving reunion of Sandor's apprentices, but her fangs were showing, she had almost reached throat-ripping-out intensity and Austin was standing within her killzone. I asked Rhetta, "When did you feel him go?"

"An hour before dark."

That matched the young man's version. "Did he have motion detectors on during the day?"

Rhetta shook her head. "That's not it. A mouse couldn't have crossed the crypt without setting off enough alarms to wake the dead... or a sleeping servant... if it was activated and set properly."

"I wasn't asleep," the servant said, "and the security system was set. I had to turn it off to let Carl go in."

Rhetta looked at me, asking, "Is he—?"

"He was staked."

She turned on the hapless boy, again, jabbing and poking at him.

"You didn't notice someone *pound*ing on the *end* of a *piece* of *wood* with a *mallet*?"

She had a nice rhythm going. You could probably dance to it. I asked, "Do you know anybody who would want to kill him?"

Rhetta's eyes widened. "No! Everybody loved him! He was wonderful!"

"Then why," Austin asked, still holding his side (The kid needed medical attention, no doubt), "were you in there last night, screaming and cursing him until he threw you out?"

200

She turned away. "It was a matter of artistic differences,"

"Since when do *artistic differences* include the words 'I'll see you staked?'"

"Children, children, children," I said. stepping between them, which was not the safest place for me to be, considering Rhetta's mood. "I need you to help me, not fight each other. I will ask the questions. You will answer them. Nobody will attack or yell—or insult, at all. If you have something to add, you will do it in a polite manner. Understood?"

"All right." I turned to Austin and asked, "Did he usually rest with any windows open?"

"Never."

"Did you leave a window open today?"

"No, sir."

"Were there any visitors last night?"

"She was here," Austin said, tilting his head in Rhetta's direction, "and then some of the Council members."

"Which members?"

"I was here, darling." The voice came from a couch in the conversation area at the other end of the studio loft.

"When did you get here, Emilia?"

Emilia Price asked, "Tonight or last night, dear?"

"Tonight."

"I brought Rhetta, poor thing." Her lethargic way of speaking hid a seldom-rivalled killing power. "She was in no condition to drive. It was the least I could do. I am the Council member for her district, precious."

"Last night?"

"I came here on Council business, with Zoltan, sweetheart," Emilia closed the distance between us. Her walk had a liquid quality, like a water bottle with a dynamite body. Wire-thin heels lifted her above my eye-level. She was sheathed in a near-black-magenta dress that was designed to stupefy. Undead certainly looked good on her.

"So," I summed up the information, "we have Sandor, Austin, Rhetta, Emilia and Zoltan here last night, enough for a square dance. Is that everybody, Austin?"

"Uh, Mr. Mitchell was here for a while, too."

"Twelve hands round, honor your partners and do-si-do," I muttered.

Rhetta's shoulders raised in a self-protecting manner. She stared at Austin as if her eyes could unleash wooden stakes at him. "Dave? Dave Mitchell was here?"

"Yes. He's been here several times in the past week."

Emilia put a hand on Rhetta's shoulder and said, "I feel the same way about him, child. Remember what they say: 'Those that can, do. Those that can't, become critics,' honey."

I turned back to Austin. "Would you have heard anyone opening a window in there?"

Before he could answer, Rhetta spoke. "No. It's soundproofed. Sandor said the silence helped his creativity as he day-slept."

"We don't—"

"I know," she said. "We don't hear anything when we're under, but it never did any good to argue with him. He always had the same answer—"

Austin said, "Oh yes—'Who has seen centuries of darkness and light? You, or me?'"

Rhetta nodded and smiled at Austin, the first smile I'd seen from her tonight.

The soundproofing explained why I hadn't heard Rhetta and Emilia come up in the elevator. I asked Austin, "Anything unusual, lately?"

"A couple of phone calls with nobody on the line and some graffiti painted on the sidewalk."

"And it said?"

"Bloodsucker."

"Not very friendly," I murmured.

"I cleaned it, scrubbed it off the best I could. I didn't want Sandor to have to see that." I remembered the discolored area by the street. A human, even a ren like Austin, probably wouldn't notice it, but I had.

I asked, "Did Sandor mention any problems to you, Emilia?"

"No, love, but he—"

The grinding noise of the freight elevator dropping from the loft level gave us all a moment of pause. I was betting that the sounds meant the dust-away crew was waiting downstairs.

Emilia continued with, "—he seldom talked about his personal issues, and we were here discussing Community matters, angel."

Rhetta asked, "Would it be all right if I went in to—to say goodbye?"

Austin looked at me, questions in his eyebrows. I handed out gloves and said, "It's still a crime scene. Don't move or take anything and tell me if you find something that's out of place or unusual."

I extended the latest in sterile-nitrile handware to Emilia, but she shook her head and said, "I've seen more than my share of these. I know what I'd see and it's not as if I had any deep attachment to him. We always traveled in different circles, sugar."

"Which means?"

She ran her wet-looking fingernails over the edges of a pedestaled statue, paying more attention to the lines in the dust than to me and said, "He was always an artist. I was always one of the patrons of the arts. I use artists to maintain my status, not because I like them, sweetness."

It's nice to know that some things can last beyond death... like class snobbery.

A distant clang let me know that the elevator had reached ground level.

"So," I asked, deciding to probe a bit, "who would take Sandor's place in your art-connoisseur circles? One of these associates of his?" I suggested, indicating the grieving rens, former and current.

"Austin, the darling boy, has some wonderful talent," Emilia stated, walking in a circle around me, carefully out of my reach, "but he lacks the excitement an artist needs to attract power and money. He might gain some allure if he were kicked, but the child still comes off as—safe. Where's the danger, my dear?"

"Rhetta?"

Emilia grimaced and said, "Her performance art is self-indulgent. She drank a pint of blood—at the blood bank—in front of an audience, which did not please the Council. We worry about exposure. Watching vampires in movies and reading about the oh-so-sexy undead is one thing. People enjoy it and pay for it, but how would the living feel if they realized that their waiter could puncture their jugulars and drain them dry before the appetizers were ready, sweetie?"

"That might make us unpopular," I admitted, "but what about Rhetta, aside from her artistic side? Would she fit your needs?"

"In many personal ways, she would. I could see her with me for quite a while," Emilia said with a sly smile, "but I have to balance the public side of her in my decision-making, angel."

"So," I recapped, "Austin is wrong because he doesn't stand out and Rhetta is wrong because she stands out."

"See," she murmured, "you do understand, *mon petit*. Of course, Rhetta might learn to—moderate her style if she had a patron who could—lead her. Don't you think so, dear?"

The whirring of a motor announced that the elevator was on its way back up to the loft, just before the chamber door slammed open.

"WHAT," demanded Rhetta, "is that THING doing in there?"

"I beg your pardon?"

"That THING on the wall."

I said, "I believe it is hanging there. It's a little bit crooked, but it is hanging."

She pointed in a general direction that might include the painting in the coffin room and stated, "It doesn't belong there. It's an affront to Sandor and everything his art represents! Why would he stick that THING where it would be the first thing he saw when he opened the lid in the evening?"

I raised my hand and said, "That's what I was wondering."

Austin said, "Sandor didn't put it there."

Rhetta wanted to know, "Then WHO did? You?"

"No," Austin said. "I didn't want it in there, so I refused to help Mr. Mitchell."

The elevator ground to a stop and the gates clanked open. Horacio and Ynez wrangled their equipment into the loft area, ordering each other around in Spanish, their coveralls emblazoned with "RAMOS CLEANING. You Do It. We Clean It."

"*Hola, Carlos*," Horacio said, smiling as he passed by and his wife nodded at me and said, "*Señor Sangre*."

I handed her the bag of dust and bone fragments and told Ynez, "*Esto es para el Consejo*." She said, "Gracias," and put the sample into a bubble-wrap-padded envelope destined for the Council Labs. She smiled at me and I could see the tips of her fangs. She continued lugging equipment toward the scene of the crime.

Rhetta grabbed Austin and he flinched; I really needed to get the boy to medical care.

She said in a near-snarl, "Why did Dave Mitchell put that thing in there?"

A voice near the elevator said, "It was a peace offering."

We turned to see the aforementioned, overstuffed art critic waddling in our direction. We really needed a people-counter to beep every time somebody entered the place.

Rhetta spat. "You blood-sucking leech."

Dave looked around the room and asked, "Aren't we all? Young Austin excepted, at the moment. Look, Sandy and I have had some differences and I was trying to make nice, give him a little present."

Austin shook his head and said, "He hated it."

Dave shrugged his fatty shoulder and said, "But it's the thought that counts, know what I mean? Now, Rhetta, a feature article before your next showing would do wonders. We could get together for a quiet interview, any time at all. What would be a good night for that?"

I was thinking that *when pigs fly*, the *Twelfth of Never*, or *the next time a politician tells the truth, the whole trut, and nothing but the truth* would be the best time for that interview, but I wasn't the one being asked the question. Instead, Rhetta explained, "I'd have to look at my schedule and get back to you," which was probably more effective than any of my answers, but not as much fun to say.

"Rhetta, my heart," Emilia said, checking the hour on her cell phone, "I must run, poopsie."

Dave humbly spread his fleshy arms and said, "If she's leaving you behind, I'd be happy to take you—anywhere."

Nothing is sadder than a bottom-feeder trying to feed at the top.

Rhetta showed great poise and told him, "No, I'll be leaving now. There is nothing more I can do for Sandor and Emilia has offered me a place to think and mourn. Shall we go, Emilia?"

The two females headed for the elevator, Emilia comforting the younger vampire. It was an interesting sight to watch, but I had questions to ask. I focused my attention on Dave.

"Mr. Mitchell," I began, "why did you need to give Sandor a peace offering?"

"You knew Sandy, right? He could get upset over nothing and hate you for a century," Dave said, his jowls jiggling. "Sometimes, I'd swear he'd get mad at me just because he couldn't think of anything else to do."

"What was it this time?"

"How should I know?"

"Perhaps," Austin offered in a low tone, "it was because Sandor didn't like Mr. Mitchell trying to make moves on Rhetta. He told you to leave her alone."

I asked, "Is that true, Mitchell?"

"Not in those exact words, but, yeah, he said, 'Leave her alone.' I guess they were his exact words, after all. He was sore about that."

I cleared my throat and asked, "Could you do something for me, Dave? That paper you write for—"

"*The Independent Tribune.*"

"Right," I said. "They have files and you have your own—personal files, I'm sure."

"Oh, indeed I do," Dave chuckled.

I ignored the smarminess. "Here's what I need. Go through those files. Look for people who have had—problems with Sandor Cusak. Arguments, disagreements, feuds, knock-down drag-outs. I need to know who hated him enough to finish him off and who knew what it took to get the job done permanently for a vampire."

"I can do that," the pudgy critic said with a self-satisfied smile.

"Good," I said, steering him toward the exit, secretly hoping he would—accidentally, mind you—drop down the shaft. "Let me know what you find."

He trundled off and I casually said to Austin, "What gets me is that somebody thought enough of him to consider turning him into a vampire, even looking and acting like that. I mean, he was a flabby, sleazy newspaperman as a human and now he's a tubby, obnoxious art critic as a vampire. Some people get kicked, but they never really change."

A far-off voice shouted, "I heard that!"

"Okay, maybe they get better hearing," I muttered and I looked at Austin. "So, why was Rhetta threatening Sandor?"

"The Council wanted her to tone down the blood elements of her performances, as usual."

"That's not the first time that's happened," I observed. "Why would that get her anger up to the I'll-see-you-staked level?"

"Maybe," Austin said, "because it was the first time Sandor threatened to cut off his support."

My eyebrows raised and I said, "That would do it."

Chapter Three
Allow Me to Introduce Myself

Horacio and Ynez were still disposing of the remains with a shop-vac when I left the loft with Austin. It was a little disturbing, knowing that your undead life wouldn't end with a bang or a whimper, but with a sucking sound.

Once the kid was safely on his way to a Community-friendly clinic by taxi, I stood at the slightly-stained curbing for a while, trying to make out the remnants of the spray-painted letters (maybe an L over here; that one could be a C), I surveyed the night around me, focusing on that building across from the fire escape. A minor temperature variation, a bump in my heat vision, one window that was slightly different and I had it pinpointed. I headed across the street, sprinting and jumping and climbing.

Minutes later, I waited, clinging to the stonework above the window like a rumpled Spider-Man, waiting until I saw a pair of binoculars slowly protrude from the opening. I flipped over the cornice and dove into the room, knocking over the less-than-muscular observer. I held him to the floor with a knee on his chest while I scanned the place.

A squatter's nest in a squat, ugly building: the room was littered with pizza boxes, take-out bags, a battery lamp and a sleeping bag on an air mattress. The place must have been an office at one time, with a pair of battered desks along one wall.

I asked my squirming new friend, "Who are you?"

He squealed, "Abomination!"

"Pleased to meet you. My name is Carl."

"You are an Abomination! Spawn of the Devil! You are Evil!" As if the words could hurt me.

"Hey, buddy." I poked him in the ribs just enough to get his attention, but not enough to skewer him, "I'm not the one doing unauthorized surveillance on law-abiding citizens. That's the government's job."

He assumed a teacher's voice, like he was explaining calculus to a third grade and stated, "I am watching the monsters to learn their weaknesses."

"Really? I have a weakness for key lime pie. Got any?"

I wasn't holding him firmly and he was still cursing me, wriggling to try and escape my "foul grasp," as he termed it. Somehow, he managed to reach into his pocket and the next thing I knew, the guy was waving a crucifix in my face, shouting, "Back, Fiend!"

"Come off it, man," I said, as I removed the cross from his hand and tossed it aside with no damage to me. "I wasn't big on religion when I was alive. It doesn't do much for me, now."

"Undead heathen!"

"Yeah, sure. That might fit. Now, let's get back to more important matters. Who are you, Mr. Abomination? What's your real name?"

"You cannot use your vampire magic on me! I will tell you nothing." He shut his eyes to scrunching-face intensity for fear that I would lo ck him into my gaze and force him to do my will.

I sighed. He'd been reading too many paranormal urban fantasy books. I was going to have to do this the hard way. He screeched in terror when I flipped him over onto his flabby little tummy. A quick pull... and I had his wallet. Along with far too many receipts from dollar stores, I found his card case.

"Good evening, Mr. Norwich... or should I call you Adam? Nice card. 'Adam L. Norwich, Vampire Hunter. Stake-Outs Our Specialty.' Cute. What does the L stand for? Louis? Lawrence?" I asked as I went through his billfold. "... Littleton?"

"How did you know?" He struggled, wanting an answer. "Bloodsucker sorcery?"

"No. I looked at your driver's license, which has expired, by the way. You'd better take care of that. You wouldn't want to be breaking the law." I leaned down and whispered, "Come on, Adam. Let's be friends."

He shouted with indignation, "You drink blood!"

"That's right. Actually, I'd love to drink synthetic blood, but that hasn't been invented in this world, only in fictional ones, so I drink the real stuff—but I'm trying to cut down," I added with a grin that was lost on him, since he was still face-down on the slightly-crunchy carpet.

"Look,"

He didn't.

"I have a few simple questions. Where should I start?" I knew what I wanted to ask, but I gave him enough time to let him think I was really thinking about it. "Oh, yes. How long have you been watching the loft?"

He didn't say anything for ten seconds, so I added a little more knee pressure, and he grunted. "Close to two weeks," which would have been my guess from the amount of trash I could see.

"I like that answer, Adam. It's honest." I patted him on the head, which ground his face a smidgen deeper into the grimy carpeting. "I like honest people. It means I don't have to get angry. When I get angry, I break things like lights—and soft things—and Peeping Toms. Let's see if your luck holds out. Don't get me angry, okay?"

"Okay," came his muffled reply.

"Next question," I announced. "What have you seen in the last few days of your covert observation?"

"Creatures of darkness," he said with disgust, "gathering and cavorting in defiance of nature and all that is holy."

Members of the Council assembled in Sandor's studio the night before, so that was probably a pretty good description of what Adam saw, allowing for exaggeration and a prejudiced observer. "I can accept that answer, but try to be a bit more objective, will you? Less editorializing and character assassination, please: just the facts. Now, who went through that window during the day?"

"Nobody."

I kicked the lamp away from the sleeping bag and the glass shattered when it bounced off the wall.

214

"Oops," I said. "I broke a lamp. I must be getting angry."

Adam Littleton Norwich whimpered.

"Let's try this again." I added a chuckle I copied from an old Richard Widmark movie. "Did you see anyone enter the window near the fire escape?"

"Tonight! The only one I saw! Honest! He came out, hung on the wall like an accursed spider and went back in," Adam said. There was a sharp breath of recognition from him. "It—It was you!"

I flexed my fingers, angling my nails into claws and slashed—the air mattress. There was a brief Bronx cheer sound, the first rush of escaping air. I'm not very intimidating to most vampires, so I get a minor dose of malicious glee out of showing off to humans—once in a while. I know it's not nice, but a guy has to have a hobby. That's why I picked Adam up off the floor, force-walked him to the window and dangled him over the street by one arm. He looked like a quivering bag of thrift-shop donations.

"Okay, here's how it goes. It's your last chance. You're getting sweaty and slippery, so I need the fastest answer you can give me. Did you see anybody else use that window?"

I let him slide half an inch to jog his memory and he screeched, "I swear! Honest! Don't kill me! You were the only one who went through! Somebody opened the window last night, but they didn't go out. They just opened it!"

That wasn't the answer I wanted, but it sounded like the truth. I thought of letting him drop on principle, just because he fancied himself the new

215

Van Helsing or a male Buffy the Vampire Slayer, but I didn't. Instead, I brought him in, laid him out on the floor next to his deflating airbed and dropped one of my business cards on his chest.

"Look," I said, "I highly recommend that you leave this building and play out your vampire-hunting games at home, where the big, bad blooddrinkers stay safely on the other side of your TV screen." I patted him on his stubbly cheek. "However. if you insist on taking a walk on the stupid side, you can get in touch with me...the info is on the card...but this is all an experience you'll want to—forget."

That mental push, the closest thing to his dreaded vampire mind tricks that I could manage, didn't erase his memories, but it fuzzed them up, made them less distinct and made him probably too confused to notice my exit out the window.

I wandered cheerfully on my way, buoyed up by the opportunity I'd had to scare the snot out of the living. I was thinking, doing my best to make sense out of the senseless and it didn't surprise me when I noticed myself standing at the door of the Express Cafe, the sweetest greasy spoon in the city—open 24/7—where I've had some of my best thoughts.

"Morning, Carlos."

"Morning, Lester," I said while I took my usual seat at the counter, the third from the far end. It didn't really matter where I sat. We were alone in the joint, but it was my favorite spot, so that's where I put myself.

"What'll it be?"

216

"The usual."

"One Cherry Dream Shake, comin' atcha," he called out and a deep-pink concoction zoomed down the counter, easing to a stop right in front of me. That's service. It was ready before I got there.

"You're a lifesaver," I sighed.

"That was a long time ago."

I took my first swig of the sweet, diluted hemoglobin. He was the one who found his favorite cop, Carlos Torres, in the alley, bleeding from multiple gunshots and—It was a mercy bite. I was going to die and my friend did what he could to help. The blood-bond was still strong, why Lester knew I was on my way before I knew where I was going.

"You look perplexed," he observed, wiping down an already-sparkling-clean counter. "The Cusak case?"

"What else?" Lester was on the Council, so he probably knew about Sandor's final death before I reached the studio loft. An African-American short-order cook might not seem the first choice for membership of the ruling legislature for the nightside of the city, but he had been around for a long, long, long time.

"Now, I have a classic, a locked-room murder, with the victim staked in broad daylight, except there's an open window. It makes sense to figure that the killer came in through the window, right?"

"It does seem logical," he mused, a smile spreading across the darkest skin I've ever seen on a vampire, "but I'm sure there's a problem, or you wouldn't be trying to suck your drink through that spoon."

"Oh. Yeah." I switched to the straw. "It seems I have a witness that says nobody went through that window."

Les swiped a sponge across the counter without much effort. "Is this a reliable witness?"

"I'd call him reliably hostile."

"All right, Carlos, tell me about it." Lester Washington looked at me the way he used to do when I was a rookie police detective, stopping in for a bite at the end of my shift. He had a way of helping me focus on the important elements, the questions I needed to answer.

"Wait a minute, Lester." I gave him my version of a steely stare, which was closer to thin-gauge copper. "You were there, last night. You're on the Council. You probably know parts of this that I don't."

"Could be," he admitted, "but let me see it through the filter of your bloodshot eyes. Tell me about it."

I started from the beginning, from Austin's call after sundown, the layout of the loft and Sandor's chamber, and the sight of the stake sticking out of The Coffin.

"Okay. Tell me about the murder weapon."

I started to examine the stake with my mind.

"It's dark, black, elegant. The top is slick and waxy. It cut through the lid and the lining, rammed all the way through Sandor's body and wedged in the coffin's bottom. The tip was cracked and shattered from the force."

"The pointed end was broken, and the top…?"

Looking at my mental image of the murder weapon, watching an imaginary arm striking it with an imaginary mallet, I said, "It was smooth! If someone pounded that shaft into the coffin and Sandor, there would be marks on the top of the stake, cracking and rough edges, but it wasn't like that! It was smooth!"

"How could that be? Did they manually insert it? That would take a lot of strength."

"It would take vampire strength, but I'm not sure I know any vampires that strong. Besides, it happened an hour before sunset. You don't find a lot of the Community out and about at that time. It can be done, but that would be a weakened, disoriented creature."

"Where is this leading you?"

"Back to Sandor's chamber."

"Not yet, Carlos. It's getting close to dawn. Go home. Get some rest. Tomorrow is another night. The puzzle will wait."

"Right." I paid for my Cherry Dream, dropped a healthy tip on the counter and left to the rhythms of Les trash-talking with the just-arrived day cook, getting ready for the morning customers.

I went home to my walk-down apartment and my police-issue coffin and tucked myself in for a long day's sleep.

Chapter Four
Wax On, Wax Off

Elevators seem to slow down the more you want to be at the end of the trip. Sandor's elevator felt like it was on a par with a narcoleptic snail dragging a bowling ball. I was ready to just climb the shaft, but the platform finally crunched and wheezed and ground to a stop.

Austin watched me stagger a little as I entered the loft. "Mist... uh... Carl, are you all right?"

"I'm fine, only frustrated at how slow the ride up here is," still at a seven on the Sangre Annoyance Scale.

"Sandor felt that way, too, sometimes. He'd leave me with the groceries and scramble up the wall," the young artist said, looking wistful, perhaps longing for paranormal abilities. "By the time I opened the gate, he'd be at work on some new painting or sculpture."

I guess I wasn't the first vampire to consider a faster mode of transportation than The Sloth Freight Express. The kid looked better than he had the last time I saw him. I told Sandor's former ren, "I need to look at his chamber again."

"It's open."

Surprised, I echoed, "It's open?"

"After the cleaners were done, a Council member told me to leave it unlocked, because 'Sandor won't be using it,'" Austin shuddered. I wouldn't be thrilled about it, either, if someone that had been a major part of my life was being treated as nothing more than a real estate vacancy.

"A Council member? Which one?"

"Zoltan."

"It figures. Zoltan is the practical one on the Council—practically without humanity—and don't quote me to anybody," I warned. I entered into Sandor's darkness and the flare of his activated lighting.

The stake lay on the platform, next to The Coffin. The ebony weapon was somewhat speckled after being dusted for fingerprints that weren't there. I still used gloves for examining crime scenes, even already-been-processed ones. The wood was smooth, except for the splintering at the tip, where it had forced its way through wood and cloth and undead flesh. The top was slick and waxy and... wax! It was topped with a layer of wax, slightly stretched at one side, like it had pulled loose from some...

I could feel a vibration in the roots of my fangs and it spread to my fingers, my feet, my body and the curtains, a rattling sound growing with it. clung to The Coffin as the impaling instrument bounced and wiggled next to me with a simulation of life until the shaking receded because the train that ran past the old factory was now far, far away. Those vibrations would shake anything loose—yeah, loose—and my derailed train of thought pulled into the station, after all.

I looked up into the blackness above me in the crypt, crouched and prepared to jump, but a guy has to know his limitations. Instead of an elegant leap, I scrambled up the curtains, hoping Sandor had bought the heavy-duty stuff. He had and the fabric held until I reached the girders, ductwork and the ceiling. I hung from the black-painted steel, inching along, examining each millimeter until, right over The Coffin, there was a blob of wax with a ragged, stretched edge—match to the one on the ebony stake—stuck under an I-beam. Aha!

With a swing and a semi-graceful drop, I returned to the floor without breaking any part of me or The Coffin. I didn't even have to pretend not to limp as I strode into the studio area. Austin was painting something delicate and precise and I didn't want to disturb him, so I waited without moving. Vampires are good at that, even if we have little patience for slow elevators, but I did start wondering when this guy was going to take a break until, "I know you're standing behind me, but I'm not quite—finished. There!" He stepped away from the canvas. I was impressed.

"Now, what is your question?"

"You told me who was here in the loft on the night before Sandor was—finished off, but there is something else I need to know. Who was in there, in his chamber, alone, with no one else?"

He cleaned his brushes before replying. Maybe Austin was choosing what to tell me and what to keep to himself, or maybe it was because he was obsessive about the cleanliness of his tools. "The Council group left before Rhetta arrived. After talking to her, Sandor left Rhetta in there to cool down. That took a while. He was in there, earlier, with Emilia for a conversation, but stomped out of

222

there, swearing in several languages. Of course, Mr. Mitchell was in there to hang that ugly thing, alone. Once he took it out of the crating and saw what it was, I refused to help him. I walked out of there, made him do it himself. It's crooked."

"I noticed."

"Emilia was by herself several minutes, until Zoltan went in to talk to her, but they left the chamber together."

I had to know. "Were you in the day-crypt alone?"

It's interesting, watching reactions to simple questions. Expressions and reactions flash across faces like people are taking a multiple-choice test. They're wondering...*Will I have the right answer, the wrong answer, or get caught cheating?* The look on Austin's face seemed to settle into a *He'll probably find out anyway, so I might as well lay it out for him* level and he gulped once before he said, "Yes. Several times. I cleaned things up, got things ready and checked on things, the way I would any other day. I was usually in and out of there lots of times a day and I never thought about it. I mean 'Sandor might get staked today, so I'd better not spend a lot of time in here' never crossed my mind."

"I'm sorry, but I needed to ask. It's my job."

"Some job."

"Tell me about it." I almost left. It was probably because I dreaded the long, slow ride to street level in the Lift That Didn't, but I asked, "What will happen to you? Will the Council let you stay here?"

"No, I have until the end of the month."

"After that?"

"I'm on my own, unless a kind-hearted, generous vampire sees fit to take a struggling artist under his wing."

I pushed my hands against air. "Don't look at me. I live in a walk-down apartment with less space than Sandor's bathroom. If I wasn't in day-sleep most of the time I was there, I could die of claustrophobia."

"I tried."

"Actually, I put in a good word for you with Emilia, but she seems to be leaning more toward Rhetta."

"I thought so."

"Her objections to you seem to come from a perception of you as being safe. You need to be—more exciting."

Austin looked down at his black outfit. "This is as exciting as I get."

"Good luck." I thought about my own just-this-side-of-scruffy look. Do I fit into the world of the rich and powerful vampires? No. How do I survive? I'm useful. Somebody has to solve the mysteries and catch the culprits. It's what I've always done and I'm not making plans to stop.

I stopped.

I knew the answer.

Chapter Five
Sharp Justice

They gathered slowly. They would have gathered faster if they had climbed the elevator shaft the way Sandor used to do, but they took the Freight Elevator That Could, Barely. They were all there.

Austin.

Rhetta.

Emilia.

Zoltan.

Horacio.

Ynez.

Dave.

Lester.

"Sangre, what is so urgent about this? There is much to be done, Council business to do, and you call us here for—What? A memorial service?" Zoltan was fuming—his default attitude.

"I'd call it a moment of justice. Suspects, observers, prosecuting detective, all assembled."

I turned to Austin.

"You were here when Sandor met his end, the only one in the loft. That gives you opportunity."

"But, I—"

"A stake plunged through his heart, as well as through the coffin that surrounded it. That would take strength—vampire strength—something you don't have. However, the murder weapon was a stake, suspended from a girder above the coffin. Could you have climbed up there and stuck it in place? Live men can't jump like a vampire can. You didn't have the means. You didn't do it."

The kid relaxed. I gazed at Rhetta. Her jaw shifted to the left, an aura of defiance in her eyes.

"Sandor threatened to stop supporting you if you endangered the Community and the Council."

"I'm an artist. I have to—"

"You don't have to. You want to. You're a spoiled brat, out to get attention."

Rhetta took a breath, ready to protest, but Emilia placed a hand on her shoulder and the young artist released the air in a measured, calming way.

"You threatened Sandor. You had motive, but you weren't alone long enough to rig a falling stake. You didn't have the opportunity."

Emilia patted Rhetta twice on the shoulder and the two shared slight smiles.

"Now, Emilia wanted Rhetta—"

Rhetta looked up at Emilia, disconcerted.

"—just because she wants anything that makes her seem more powerful and she looked down on Sandor. Motive. Of course, she looks down on everybody. She could have done it, but she would never have gone to all that trouble, just to get rid of someone. She had other ways of getting what she wanted. She had motive and means, but she didn't care enough to kill."

Rhetta edged two baby-steps away from Emilia. Emilia noticed.

"Zoltan was never alone in the chamber, so he had no opportunity."

226

I looked at Dave. So did everybody else. His eyes widened as it dawned on him that he stood in the center of a circle.

"You think I--?"

"Sandor warned you to stay away from Rhetta. Your 'peace offering' came boxed, a box that easily held a wooden stake. I'll give you credit for making it out of ebony. That had style. It also hid the weapon when you waxed it to the metalwork in the darkness over the coffin. The vibrations of the passing trains loosened the wax until the stake fell on your sleeping victim. You even opened a window to make it look like someone entered from outside the building. You didn't know a wannabe vampire hunter watched from across the street, a witness who saw it."

Dave looked to his left, toward the elevator, then looked in other directions with faster movements. We definitely surrounded him, and the circle grew tighter.

I polled the jury

Horacio—*"Culpable."*

Ynez—*"Culpable."*

Zoltan—"Guilty."

Emilia—"Guilty."

Rhetta—"Guilty."

Austin—"Guilty."

Lester—"Guilty.

Carlos- "Guilty."

Horacio and Ynez took hold of Dave's arms. He whimpered. The cleaners bared their fangs and bit him. Each member of the circle took a turn, taking a sip of his blood. Austin—who had no fangs—hesitated, but Rhetta guided him in taking a lick from one of the streams of red.

I reached behind a table, brought out the ebony stake used to kill Sandor and a mallet from the sculpting tools in the loft. I handed the stake to Rhetta and gave the mallet to Austin.

Rhetta placed the now- sharpened point against Dave's chest. Austin took a deep breath. He swung the mallet with all his force. Blood sprayed as the stake pierced through cloth, skin, fat, and ribcage into the heart.

Horacio and Ynez let go of the arms they had held. Dave's pudgy body crumpled. Flesh liquified into a sludgy mass. Time and decay are relentless.

Rhetta reached out and embraced Austin. They held each other tightly. I hoped that didn't re-injure his ribs. She released him and led him toward Sandor's chamber, past Emilia, who turned and shrugged at me. "Dave always had bad taste. I didn't know he'd taste bad, too."

Emilia nodded at Zoltan and they headed for the freight elevator.

The chamber door closed behind Sandor's former rens. They had things to talk about, fences to mend, plans to make. There was hope.

I looked at Horacio and Ynez, standing there in their work uniforms.

"Sorry about leaving you to clean up the mess."

"You did your job, *Señor Sangre*. We will do ours."

I cringed a little when I heard the whine of the electric bone saw. Lester chuckled and we moved away from the clean-up zone.

"You look like you could use a Cherry Dream Shake."

"I think I could."

"Tell you what—I'll add a little extra A-Positive."

The Boundary Waters
Brooke MacKenzie

June 6th, 1993
7:45 AM

I will spare you the formality of "Dear Diary" and simply introduce myself. My name is Kyle, and this is the journal I will be using to record my various observations, thoughts and assorted data as I begin my new job as a ranger-slash-environmental scientist in the Boundary Waters Canoe Area—a nature preserve that begins in northern Minnesota and extends up into Canada. In the last few days, I have permanently shed my academic cloak and identity as a professor of Forest Science at Humboldt State University in Northern California and donned the rugged fabrics of the outdoor explorer. It is my hope that these pages will serve as efficient record keeping as I communicate various findings with the Forest Service. However, it is my more secret hope that these pages will be entertaining and illuminating enough to eventually morph into a memoir that people will want to read. At least those individuals who, like me, find nature to be endlessly fascinating. A fount of inspiration. Ambrosia for the Muse. Others, of course, will have no interest whatsoever. To each his own.

The next two weeks will be spent in trainings, tours of campgrounds and plenty of forced social interactions with the other ranger trainees. I will tolerate these activities to the best of my ability, knowing that my reward is the nature-drenched solitude that awaits.

June 20th, 1993
7:45 AM

The knowledge I have acquired over the past two weeks about the Boundary Waters has engendered more than feelings of awe within me. I now have a reverence for this place that borders on religious fanaticism. I have devoured information about its flora and fauna, its resilient ecosystems, its topography and its water health. It is one of very few places in America where human disruption is kept to a minimum: campers portage in with their supplies and portage everything back out again. Campsites are simple and consist solely of a fire pit, a sturdy branch or beam for hanging the food pack and, some distance away from a cleared area where the tents would be pitched, a chemical toilet known as "the throne." The throne resembles a tree stump in its height, shape and color. Everything is meant to be left completely pristine. Other than ashes, fish skeletons from a freshly caught meal and whatever is deposited into the throne, no waste of any kind can be left behind. It is a place utterly void of wanton consumption and harmful disposal.

After sunset the forest becomes so thick with mosquitos that one can scarcely see three feet in front of one's nose. All of the ranger trainees beat a retreat to the cabins that have served as our temporary home for the last two weeks, lest we be devoured by a cloud of biting insects. This early forced dispersal and natural endpoint of socializing suits me just fine. I have engaged in a few perfunctory card games with the others, but for the most part I am happy being left to my books.

Tomorrow I will find out my first set of tasks, as well as the area that I will inhabit for the next few weeks. My feelings of excitement and anticipation will no doubt prevent me from sleeping deeply tonight.

June 21st, 1993
7:45 AM

My first assignment: collecting water, algae and animal scat samples for the next two weeks at Lake Alice—one of the numerous lakes that comprise the Boundary Waters. Something seems to be disrupting the ecosystem there, resulting in such symptoms as discolored water, strange bird migration patterns and animal behavior, and unexplained fish fatalities. The ever-faithful beavers that typically populate Lake Alice in high numbers also seem to have migrated to other lakes. I certainly have my work cut out for me. It had been an unusually wet spring with record levels of rainfall. My initial thoughts, of course, are that this excess rain has thrown a monkey wrench into Lake Alice's particular ecology. The fact that surrounding lakes seem to be unaffected, however, serves to deepen the mystery. Perfect. A worthy challenge, right out of the gate.

Lake Alice is perhaps one of the most difficult lakes to get to from the Boundary Waters entry point at the aptly (but unimaginatively) named Lake One, where the ranger cabins are located. While this means more exertion in terms of paddling and portaging, the benefit is that it will be sparsely populated by campers. This should make for an easier and more focused research experience, as part of my job in the hybrid role of ranger-slash-researcher is, of course, to monitor the campers. Or, if I am choosing to not mince words, to babysit them. The fewer the campers, the fewer the headaches. I was never destined for au pair work.

It will take me two days to reach Lake Alice if I paddle from dusk to dawn. I'd be remiss if I did not mention the fact that I am dreading the numerous portages between lakes that will require me to get out of my canoe and carry it, along with my gear, for several hundred rods (in case you didn't know, Dear Reader, a rod is a unit of measurement equal to the length of a canoe, or approximately 16 feet). But these are the less pleasant aspects that must be endured for peace and quiet. The fact that I will have to traverse six different lakes before reaching Lake Alice also means that I will be able to collect ample samples from these lakes for comparison with the water in Alice. Silver linings abound. I leave tomorrow at dawn.

June 24th, 1993
6:00AM

I have made it to Lake Alice, not without mishaps. One of the portages had completely washed away from a particularly destructive storm earlier in the spring, which meant having to wade through knee-deep mud while dragging my canoe and supplies behind me like a wretched pack mule. A full and unopened bottle of cooking oil—a vital supply for surviving on walleye and northern pike, as well as for heating up freeze-dried delicacies— was jettisoned from my pack unbeknownst to me at some point during my journey. Luckily I happened to pack a spare—not all the way full, but it will last if I ration it—without even remembering having done so. It was as if my baser instincts had appealed to some part of my brain while packing, predicting somehow that such a thing would be needed. I was grateful my brain had listened.

The entry point to Lake Alice from the gut-wrenching 270 rod portage is reedy and coated in algae, but after paddling through the morass I was greeted with a surprisingly vast, lapis-hued expanse of lake. It was far larger than I had envisioned after studying it on the map, and its shape seemed more round and gentle on the eye than I had anticipated. Its shoreline displayed a smattering of diversity that I reasoned might be mirrored by the ecosystem in and around the lake itself: collections of dense pine trees standing rigidly at the very edge of the lake, craggy rock face cliffs, and even stretches of sandy beach. There were plenty of attractions to keep a variety of animal inhabitants happy: an excess of wood for the beavers and muskrats; shallow, reedy wading areas for the moose; tangles of wild berry bushes for the black bears and, judging by the number of loons bobbing and diving on the lake's surface, plenty of fish. Clearly the number of fish fatalities reported by my colleagues had not been enough to deter the loons. I followed the map to the dot my supervisor had circled in pen, indicating the campsite I was assigned to during my stay at the lake. It was, of course, all the way across the lake from the entry point, which meant that my scrawny academician arms would continue to receive a hearty wilderness workout from paddling.

I made quick work of setting up camp: locating the throne, pitching my tent, unpacking supplies and hanging the food pack from the designated tree limb that would be out of reach from bears. The sun was beginning to think about dipping below the horizon and I wanted to paddle my canoe around the lake to collect my first sample—and possibly a fish— before dark. I managed both in quick succession, and so I decided to troll around so that I could begin a sketch of the lake in my notebook. I was able to make satisfactory progress on the sketch until the forest became a cacophony of mosquito buzzing. It was alarming just how loud the dull roar was, even from the middle of the lake. As I reached shore, I steeled myself to run through the curtain of bugs, shielding my eyes with my hand as I did and diving headfirst into my tent. Whilst I was able to spot and kill the few stragglers that had been able to take advantage of the brief unzipping of the tent flap, I can only hope that I have not inadvertently left a solitary mosquito alive, humming in its melancholy, to feast on me during the night.

2:45 AM

I am awake. The layer of sleep that coats me tonight is thin and liquid and accompanied by a matching layer of sweat on my skin. I am awake because of a sound. It is almost as if the pitch of the mosquitos has changed. The whine seems to have descended dramatically into a deep, whirring moan. I can feel the ground vibrating ever so slightly, even through the layers of my air mattress and sleeping bag. The sound is both ubiquitous and consistent: it is not the sporadic, guttural sound of growling bears roaming the nocturnal landscape for food. It is everywhere at once. It sounds almost mechanical. Steady and perpetual. Surely there is a logical explanation—it is the sound of something manmade and exploitative of/disruptive to the natural surroundings of the Boundary Waters. I will explore further in the morning. For now my only response is to fight for a few more hours of sleep before daylight.

June 25th, 1993
9:20 PM

I spent the morning exploring the woods around my campsite in an effort to locate the sound from last night. So far it remains elusive. I ventured out into the lake to collect samples from several different locations, which I have dutifully documented on my hand-drawn map. After lunch my supervisor contacted me on the walkie-talkie and asked me to inspect a campsite that hadn't fared well in the wet spring weather. The fire pit had washed away entirely and the throne had suffered a gruesome flooding episode. I spent some time exploring the woods around the site and couldn't help but notice a quiet that permeated the woods. The air was absent of birdsong and even the whistle of wind. Only the sound of my footsteps through the undergrowth disrupted the stark silence. I ventured deeper into the woods to look for scat samples to collect—those delightful treasure troves of information about the health of both an individual animal as well as an environment—but saw none. This was surprising, as this particular section of forest was a buffet of plant, bark and berry delicacies that would appeal to black bears, moose and even smaller rodents. And yet, it all seemed to be untouched. I took some extra water samples from the shoreline in this area to see if the answers were contained in water. So far, all answers to my questions have remained out of reach. I am unsettled by the silence.

After communicating my various findings— and lack thereof—via walkie-talkie to my colleagues, I spent some time trolling around the perimeter of the lake in my canoe so I could add more detail to my notebook map sketch. A pair of loons followed me for the duration of my journey, their sleek obsidian bodies peppered with pure white. They moved with purpose, perfectly engineered for their surroundings and supporting role in nature and eyed me with an astute mixture of curiosity and suspicion.

After over an hour of paddling, I found a deep spot in the lake below a rock face that rose no more than eight feet out of the water and decided to strip down to my underwear and make it my own personal diving platform. I was fairly confident that no humans or animals would be alarmed by my whoops of delight as I jumped, cannonballed and swan dove to my heart's content. Even the loons stayed put and acted as my captive, if thoroughly unimpressed, audience.

The rock face with its granitic properties and quartz and feldspar flecks took on a subtly pleasant sheen in the late afternoon sun and when it did, I noticed something unexpected: the entire rock face—from the very top to the water level—was covered with small carvings. They were subtle and so numerous that they had simply blended in at first and I really had to look to see them. The Boundary Waters is certainly home to many Native American pictographs that have been carved and painted on a variety of surfaces. These, however, were less pictograph and more geometric shapes and straight lines intersecting at various angles, almost like Runic letters (though having studied the Runic alphabet, I could say with confidence that they were not). Given their definition in the rock, these appeared to be fairly recently created. Based on their number and clean precision, I could deduce that they would have taken a long time to carve into the rock. I ran my wet hand over them, darkening them slightly. The best conclusion I could draw was that the carvings were the work of some bored campers with fancy knives. *Overly outfitted and underly sensible*, my supervisor liked to say about far too large a percentage of Boundary Waters visitors. And while I could see how a camper would have managed to make a carving at the water level and at the top of the small cliff, I couldn't figure out how the carvings in the middle had been made. It simply defied logic, because there was no stable surface on which to stand in order to reach the places where the carvings had been made. I paddled back to camp, noticing a strange humming sensation in the hand that had touched the carvings. I also noticed an unsettled sensation in my stomach. Strange.

When I got back to my campsite, I saw a tree near my tent quaking, as if it had just been disturbed by an animal or bird making a hasty getaway upon my arrival. Perhaps there are signs of life after all.

3:05 AM

It is the middle of the night and I have been stirred awake by noises in the forest behind my tent. It is cloudy so the stars and moon are of no assistance to my vision. I am puzzled by these noises. They are not the telltale crashing of black bears, moose, or anything else that might be foraging at night. While I hear trees being jostled and undergrowth being crushed, the sounds are traveling rapidly. If I strain my ears and keep listening, I can hear a distinctive "pitter-patter" in its movement. My ears continue to adjust and listen and I am certain I am hearing the sound of bipedal feet hitting the ground. Something is running through the forest in the pitch dark with surprising agility. And it is doing so while upright on two legs.

I am racking my brain but do not know what could be making these noises. Even humans cannot so lithely maneuver a dark forest without a light source and I can tell that there are no flashlight beams zigzagging in a telltale fashion through the trees. I must collect my courage and go out to investigate.

3:20 AM

I could see nothing outside of my tent, despite having called out and directed my flashlight into the forest. However, the voracious biting of the mosquitos made it difficult to stay out there. I will not be able to sleep as long as these noises surround me. My brain continues picking and prodding the air for clues; my senses have heightened. I've turned on my lantern and will busy myself with reading and writing until I can draw a satisfactory conclusion or the sounds stop. Whichever occurs first. I am hoping for the latter.

3:47 AM

I am writing down what I saw a moment ago. It is my hope that in writing it down my brain can process what I have just seen and then break it down into logical pieces with the end goal of making sense of it all. Because, it currently does not make sense to me. I am hoping that the culprit is lack of sleep, but I am uncertain.

I was unable to reason with my very full bladder any longer, so I affixed a headlamp to my forehead and walked a few paces from my tent to relieve myself. Just beyond the aura of light, out of my peripheral vision, I saw something begin to emerge from the forest and walk toward me. It was tall, on two legs and, for a brief second, I thought it was a bear standing erect and sniffing the (urine-soaked) air as they do. But as I turned to look directly at it, I saw the figure was distinctly human. It was not wearing clothes that I could make out in that moment and its skin looked gray and almost shimmering in my flashlight beam. A hoarse cry leapt from my throat before I could stop it. And then it was gone. It took me a moment to catch my breath (and wipe the urine from my underwear). With great caution, I walked to where it had been standing to examine for footprints. There were none.

I, of course, made a beeline for my tent and my heart and breath have finally returned to their normal rates. I know two things for certain: 1.) sleep will most definitely be non-existent tonight, 2.) I do not tend to imagine things, nor do my eyes tend to play tricks on me. Many years of studious nighttime observations have trained my brain to report accurately in limited light. My assuredness in this fact about myself and faith in my almost superhuman rationality and sensual acuity, bring me little comfort tonight.

June 26th, 1993
2:30 PM

I have a strange mark on my right arm, two purple semicircles that resemble a bite. The few minutes of sleep I did manage to get last night were restless and filled with vivid, violent dreams. It would not be entirely surprising if I had managed to bite myself in my sleep.

This morning I went fishing at dawn. The number of loons floating on the surface of the lake seems to have multiplied, which I did not think would bode well for my chances of catching breakfast, due to competition. Happily, I was proven wrong and returned to my campsite with two corpulent walleye. After going through the motions of skinning, fileting, dipping in breading and frying (once again I thanked the fates that they had not left me completely without cooking oil), I plated up the fish with a helping of Hash Browns O'Brien—a Northwoods specialty—and cocked my ear to listen. Once again, the usual campground sounds were absent. The lack of bird and assorted small woodland creature sounds is unsettling. Truly. Plus, as I learned last night, my brain is beginning to conjure up sounds and images to fill the blank spaces where the familiar sights and sounds of the forest should be. After much thought and reflection, I am beginning to think that my strange hallucination last night was just that: a hallucination. Since there were no footprints or other evidence that anyone had actually been there, I can only draw the conclusion that my imagination is running uncharacteristically wild at the moment. It is nothing more.

3:00 PM

After eating my fill and drinking grainy coffee, I needed to make my way to the throne. I walked in the forest and a new detail revealed itself to me. I'll admit, it made my heart speed up for a moment: Carved into the trunks of the birch trees that lined the short pathway were, directly at my eye level, more of the symbols that I had seen in the rock face the day before. I tried to rack my brain and dig into the more moss-covered, unconscious regions of my memory to see if these symbols had been stored there without my conscious mind noticing. I thought I would have noticed them earlier, as they were somewhat dramatic and certainly out of place, but perhaps they escaped my attention. My senses seem to be dulling as I spend more time in the deathly quiet forest. Either way there seems to be a bit of a lose-lose scenario: my senses cannot fully be trusted, or someone was wandering around near my tent and carving these shapes while I attempted to sleep.

Though I am loath to do it, I am realizing I need to search for other people in the forest, while doing my best to remain unseen by them. This was information that would be needed by the other rangers. If their penchant toward vandalism was any indication, these people are up to no good. And they were adept with a knife and apparently able to move around expertly in the dark without using flashlights.

I dread the idea of going hunting for humans. Or, as the case may be, if my suspicions are correct, I dread being some kind of potential prey for them. I would much rather take my chances with bears or moose or the occasional hungry wolf pack that wanders down this way from Canada. If there really is a roving band of people inhabiting these woods, would this also explain the absence of animals? This does not seem scientifically plausible. But then again, I am not sure what I am dealing with here. I must pluck up my courage. Here goes.

6:30 PM

It is now dinnertime and the mosquitos are beginning their discordant fugue. I searched the woods for several hours and found nothing. No footprints, no fresh campfire ashes, no tents, no discarded fish bones. It was as if whoever had been in the forest had simply vanished. But where could they possibly go? I must take a small swig of bourbon that I keep hidden in a flask at the bottom of my backpack for just such emergencies as these. My nerves are fraying like damp rope that has been overly burdened by a too-heavy food pack. What I wouldn't give to hear a woodpecker boasting its labors as it pecks loudly and routinely. Or the *churr-churring* of aggravated squirrels or darting and rustling of efficient scavengers. Even the typically loquacious loons have fallen silent. For now, all I hear is the rumbling of my own stomach and the frantic skittering of my own unreliable thoughts.

Tonight I will keep my lantern illuminated and ensure that my bladder is fully emptied before dark.

3:30 AM

I succumbed to sleep quickly and easily, even in a well-lit tent, but have now been startled awake by a sound emanating from the lake: loons. Their calls alternate between legato peaks and valleys and a frenetic staccato. It is haunting and otherworldly, but I find myself settled by it, as it is a thoroughly natural sound. There are, from what I can hear outside, dozens of them, with more pairs of wings flapping overhead, joining them. While I am delighted that the loons have regained their voices, I must admit that a large and boisterous gathering such as this is not typical loon behavior. An investigation is in order.

The loons are swimming in perfectly spaced concentric circles. But the lake. I can hardly believe I'm about to write these words. I must, partly because I doubt the reality of what I have seen and will want documentation to return to later when I am questioning my memory and my senses. The lake is glowing. And the loons swim like devoted dervishes on its surface, swirling and circling. It is Illuminated in green. Is it from beneath? Is there some kind of bioluminescent phenomenon that can explain it? Perhaps the Northern Lights have started early and they are splashing their reflection across the surface of the lake. However, the sky is dark and void of stars.

I want to stay in my tent. I should stay in my tent. I should. But now a strange compulsion to investigate is buzzing in the back of my brain like a stray mosquito. I must see what is happening.

June 28th, 1993
11:50 AM

I am trying to remember but my memories are just a dark void in my head. I remember that two nights ago I stood at the edge of the lake, watching the birds and the glowing water. I have been trying to piece together what happened next. The next thing I knew I found myself standing in the middle of the woods without remembering how I got there. I could once again hear footsteps running in the forest all around me but could see nothing, especially since I had no flashlight. It was hard to breathe and my body was twitching in its 'fight or flight' panic, but somehow my brain was subdued and I could not connect the two in order to move. I felt dizzy and nauseated and grabbed a tree to steady myself. My hand landed on another carving. When it did, an image exploded in my head. It was one that I couldn't decipher or make sense of and my gut roiled with a strange and primal knowing that it did not originate from me. There is no other way to describe it. It was someone else's thought from someone else's mind. I felt disoriented and oddly violated; I shook my head the way I would when trying to force water out of my ear. But I couldn't shake it loose. And I have now come to realize that it was only the first in a series of foreign thoughts that have been force-fed into my head. It is the vandalism of my mind. The desecration of my mental space, which has been too great for me to bear.

After that first inexplicable image subsided, a stream of stringy vomit ejected itself from my mouth and I fell to the ground. That same low humming sound from the first night radiated from everywhere and nowhere in particular. I looked around for familiar foliage and realized that I was in the woods a few feet away from the top of the rock face with the strange carvings. The same one where I had so blissfully jumped and dived only a few days earlier. Because I had no equipment, I would have to wait until daybreak to find my way back to camp. I was too weak and not in proper command of my mental faculties to attempt to return at night. I sat against the trunk of a tree, brought my knees against my chest and rested my head on them. I pinched my eyes shut and covered my ears. I didn't want to hear the footsteps or the humming and, as time passed, they jumbled into one singular sound and then everything went silent. So silent, in fact, that it was as if the sound, or any other sound for that matter, had never existed in these woods. It was as if I had made them up completely. I shivered in my fear and exhaustion and the uncharacteristically chilled air until finally dawn broke.

When I could see more clearly, I looked down at my forearm where there was a stinging sensation.

My entire body had been a veritable symphony of sensation the night before and so I hadn't thought much of my arm at first. But the stinging didn't subside the next morning and soon I understood why. On the inside of my arm, from my wrist to the crevice of my elbow, were seven evenly spaced round marks. I ran my fingers over them. They were not raised and too uniformly shaped to be insect bites. I had to fight an urge to cry as I examined them. As I looked more closely, they appeared to resemble the phases of the moon. I did not understand how I could have ended up in the middle of the woods with unexplained marks on my body. I wanted to get back to my tent—back to that small waterproof square of this forest over which I had complete control.

It seemed to take forever to get back to my campsite. I couldn't stop shivering. As I walked, my teeth chattered as if I was stranded in the arctic and not by a lake in the summer.

When I finally reached my tent, I grabbed the radio and thought about sending a message to the other rangers. But what would I say, exactly? If I told them what had happened, they would assume that I was having some kind of psychotic break from the solitude and would not be able to handle life in the Boundary Waters. And maybe they would be right. But I couldn't lose this job. I set down the radio, wriggled into my sleeping bag and slept, dreamlessly, until the next day.

June 29th, 1993
11:50 AM

I have promised myself that tomorrow after getting some rest I will begin my journey back to Lake One.

Today more thoughts are being placed in my head. It started after I touched the symbol on the tree. I do not know where they are coming from. I just know that they are becoming more and more intrusive. Images, alive in technicolor, defile and distract my thoughts. Shapes and faces and animals and snapshots of both gory scenes and growing things. I struggle to remember the individual pieces of the flashing sideshow when it is over. I only know that it is intended to convey destruction and salvation in equal portions. It is intended to activate the entire range of my emotions. It is meant to show me the meaning of something that I cannot yet decipher.

My appetite is elusive. Taking down the food pack is not worth the herculean effort. I have to gather some final water samples before departing, which is the only task that keeps me from fleeing right now. I have to respond to my supervisor's calls on the walkie-talkie and force my voice to stay casual. I have to leave my tent. But it is hard to move. My body craves sleep in a way it never has before. My joints have become somehow made of metal—stiff and so heavy. It is hard to move. In fact, it is impossible. I just need to sleep. I think if I sleep for just a little while I will feel better and can finish my tasks and prepare to leave. I am hearing rustling and footsteps outside of my tent. I know that it is not a bear. My marks on my arm throb and pulse. I need sleep.

June 30th, 1993
10:00 PM

I managed to sleep for the entire day yesterday, all through the night and throughout the day today. It is now night and I was able to muster the energy to light a fire. I sit inside my tent and watch the walls for shadows and silhouettes. I have the feeling that I am waiting for something. There are no loon calls tonight. There are no sounds at all, in fact. Once again the lake is plunged into utter silence. I am waiting. I can only hear my own ragged and exhausted breath. I am watching. It is hard to stay patient. I want to jump in my canoe and paddle away. But something inside of me is telling me to sit still. I cannot tell if this thought originated from my brain or someone else's.

3:30 AM

I am not surprised when I hear the footsteps emerging from the forest, but it does not keep me from feeling terror, nonetheless. I am both terrified and paralyzed and this combination runs counter to my survival instincts. The leaden knowledge of this settles deeply into my gut, further rooting me in the ground, making me immobile. The spots on my arm are throbbing.

The footsteps are walking and there are many of them. They enter the campsite and surround my tent, projecting their shadows against it. My body has the urge to flee, to bolt, to get in the canoe and not stop paddling until I have reached another lake. But my brain suppresses it. My brain no longer feels like mine any longer.

I can see the outlines of the figures clearly now. The shadows distort them, making their bodies appear slender and their heads appear bulbous. My brain is like a seated and loyal dog, waiting for either a treat or command from its trainer.

The shadows have just moved closer, looming larger and darker on the walls of the tent. I wait to hear them speak, to make any sort of sound, but they stay silent. They do not need to speak. They do not owe me any information. I am not worthy of it. By pure chance, I just happened to be here on their lake. But I know they have a plan for me.

A final thought wedges itself in my brain like an exclamation and remains there longer than the flashing, ephemeral others. It is a message about the Boundary Waters. One that we ignore at our peril. This place with its rugged nature, azure lakes, and various precious forms of life. The Boundary Waters must remain. At all cost, it must remain.

They want me to prepare. To be still, stop writing, and wait. Farewell, Dear Reader. They are coming for me.

Meet the Authors

Dorothy Davies is an editor, writer, photographer and medium. Somehow all these things come together in her seemingly crowded leisure and work life. She retired from editing for a while to run a second hand shop, the best one on the Isle of Wight, but the thrill of finding and publishing outstanding stories became too much so she started again with the Gravestone Press imprint. She still runs the shop...Her book, The Skullface Chronicles, the story of a zombie taking revenge on his dysfunctional family, is available through fiction4all.com. She has a store of short stories, some of which are finding their way into the anthologies, having not seen daylight for many a long year. She also channels books from spirit authors, notable figures from history. These can be found on the fiction4all.site under Zadkiel Publishing.

Paul Edwards is a life-long horror fan and writes his own twisted tales in any spare time that he can grab. He has seen three collections of stories published – Now That I've Lost You (Screaming Dreams), Black Mirrors (Rainfall Books) and Night Voices (Demain Publishing), the latter being a joint-collection with author Frank Duffy. Paul is also a fan of role-playing games, rock music and rough Somerset cider.

R W Goldsmith spent over a decade and a half as an award-winning scriptwriter for his California based wild-west re-enactment/stunt troupe. After hanging up his guns, he switched to writing science fiction, fantasy and horror novels with an occasional short story thrown in for good measure. In 2020, he served as president of The Horror Writers Association's San Diego chapter. His short stories have met with success and his post-apocalyptic dark-fantasy novel, The Serpents of Eden, was scheduled for publication in 2021 until the publisher became another statistic of the pandemic.
Visit his website at:
https://www.richardwgoldsmith.com

Terrance V. Mc Arthur is a storyteller, puppeteer, magician, basket maker and retired librarian, living in the Central Valley of California with his wife, daughter, and the cremains of a cat who lived for 21 years. Terrance's stories have appeared in Thirteen O' Clock Press anthologies.

Brooke MacKenzie is a scary movie fanatic and writes horror fiction by candlelight. Her first book, Ghost Games, will be published later in 2021 by Dreaming Big Publications. She received a B.A. from Sarah Lawrence College and an Ed.M. from the Harvard Graduate School of Education. Her writing has appeared in several places, including Who Knocks? Magazine and The Dead Games: A Zimbell House Anthology. She is the current Board Chair of the New York Writers Coalition, the largest community-based writing organization in the country. She lives in Northern California with her husband and daughter.

Visit her website: bamackenzie.com

Edward R. Rosick is an author living in the urban wilds of southern Michigan. He has attended both the Taos Toolbox and Clarion Writer's Workshops and his stories of horror and speculative fiction have appeared in numerous magazines and anthologies, including Pulphouse, Sick Cruising, and The Half That You See. His first horror novel, entitled Deep Roots, is scheduled to be published by Thurston Howl Publications.

David Turnbull is a member of the Clockhouse London group of genre writers. He writes mainly short fiction and has had numerous short stories published in magazines and anthologies. His stories have previously been featured at Liars League London events and read at other live events such as Solstice Shorts and Virtual Futures. He was born in Scotland, but now lives in the Catford area of London. He can be found at www.tumsh.co.uk.